flames of grace

An adventure of spirit

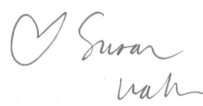

flames *of* grace

An adventure of spirit

Susan Walker

Based on a true story

Sacred Flame
PUBLICATIONS

Sacred Flame Publications
PO Box 3077
Sedona, AZ 86340

FIRST EDITION

Cover design by Kathryn Walker
Cover photograph, *Epiphany*, of author cleansed in mud, by Michele Muir
Type and layout by Karen Reider

Library of Congress Catalog Card Number: 98-96184

ISBN 0-9663891-0-7

 Printed on recycled paper.

For Lisa Maria Waikalani
whose brilliance graces this story and my life,

And for the flame that burns in every soul,
longing to know the truth.

I do not pretend to understand the Divine.

I have only glimpsed a sliver of the vastness that exists.

The following is an account of nine months of my journey.

Names and details have been altered to disguise certain
individuals and to help the story flow more smoothly.

I write of this adventure with the prayer it will remind all of us that
truth is all we have, faith is all we need and love is all there is.

This is not a story of pure truth, faith and love.
It is a quest filled with brilliant miracles and tremendous torment,
outrageous faith and overwhelming trials. It is a passionate search for
truth in which I feared I was giving up everything for nothing, only to
discover that I gave up nothing for everything.

I believe we all share the same journey.

May you see your story in mine.

With love,
I dedicate this *book* to my mom and dad,

While I dedicate my *life*
to the Mother and Father of All Things.

contents

Introduction

adventures of a displaced princess

the flames in the storm

grace unveiled

121

the blessings of england

167

enraptured in emptiness

177

reflections three years later

185

Introduction

Days before this story began, on a spring morning, I sat looking out at the patches of snow that wound around the sprawling sage brush and sturdy cedar trees of the high mountains of northern New Mexico. For three years, I had been following the call of spirit and had become accustomed to living in a sea of adventure rich with lessons, love, challenge and change.

Only three years earlier, a tiny voice inside my heart had cried to know a world beyond the physical. The voice was almost inaudible, yet it burned unceasingly in the depths of my soul. In my first major act of faith, I left my professional job fundraising millions of dollars for charity to honor my heart. Soon my life began evolving around morning meditations where I discovered that a brilliant world lay in the stillness.

In quiet moments of meditation, I first began to sense, then hear and eventually see the world of spirit. Soon I found myself regularly communing with beautiful guides and angels in the etheric plane that accompanied me on my very physical journey. In my meditations, these beings usually appeared as light in the form of a man or woman or as a ray of color. They spoke to me through a knowing in my soul, a flash of passion in my heart and in a silent language I learned to decipher. The communion was a simple process that only required the courage to believe.

In time, I discovered that in moments of confusion, I could turn to the etheric world and instantly be lead to clarity. In moments of terror, I was soothed, and in those of longing I was filled. I came to understand that the blessings of spirit were always available if I became quiet enough to hear the call and courageous enough to follow.

Through my meditations, the angels offered assistance in various realms. They gave me lessons of eternal truth and guidance to find work. They showed me the domain of pure love and helped me traverse the land of duality. While their world was filled with light, mine was a blend of the absolute miracles and the outrageous trials of the spiritual journey.

As I stumbled down my path with the conscious awareness of grace, the guides that surrounded me radiated a love that never wavered or demanded. Regardless of my actions and seemingly endless faults, they saw the beauty in my imperfections and the sweetness in my shortcomings. They only approached me, taught me and showered me with love. I never feared them, although I was often intimidated by their suggestions which challenged me to move beyond my self-imposed limitations. However, the brilliance of the connection itself always inspired me to have faith, the communion bathed me in comfort, and their energy reminded me that the Divine watches over every instant of existence.

I followed the path of spirit as best I could, even amidst moments of doubt and terror. I had been raised as an atheist, and it was not without struggle, hesitation and pain that I peeled away my ingrained beliefs. My fear would rage every time I took a step toward spirit, and in those moments, it seemed that I would die if I followed the voice of my soul, yet deep inside, I knew that I would die if I did not.

After three years of honoring the call of spirit, I was twenty-seven years old and living in northern New Mexico. I had a wonderful job as the marketing and publicity director of a small book publishing company, I had been offered a beautiful home to live in for free, and my life was filled with friends who inspired me to create, heal and be true to myself.

One spring morning, as I acknowledged the incredible grace that engulfed my life, I once again felt a yearning in my heart that desperately cried for more. I gazed out onto the beauty of the high desert and realized that I still felt separate. Suddenly, it was no longer enough that I could commune with the world of spirit. I longed for greater union.

I contemplated the desire that tore at my heart, and the following poem erupted from the depths of my being. It flowed forth with abandon, and it summarized my state:

As I sit in a beautiful adobe home with a fire burning behind me
  and a stream running beside me, I know I want more than I feel
  at this moment.
Overwhelming beauty does not stir the depths of my soul,
  Unless I become one with the beauty.
The passion of the fire does not reach deep inside of me,
  Until I reach deep inside of it.
And the melody of the stream does not sing to my heart,
  Until the voice of my heart sings to the stream.

It is the awareness of separation that leads me to the longing
  for union.
I no longer want to see the flame,
  I want to be the flame.
I am no longer content to lie beside the melodious stream,
  I yearn to have the water flow through me.
And the earth itself in all of Her brilliance
  Only soothes me if I rest within Her.

My longing is for union.
Complete, full and never-ending union.
For all else is simply illusion,
And I long for truth.

The world of spirit gave me a simple yet mysterious response to the prayer of my poem. I set down my pen, and as sweetly as mist falls upon the dry desert, I heard the words, "Commune with the Divine Mother."

The suggestion left me baffled. I had never heard of the concept of the Divine Mother, so I settled into meditation to ask for more information. To my surprise, as I closed my eyes and came into the center of my being, I saw only darkness. I concentrated more intensely and waited for an answer, yet all I heard was the crackle of the fire and the wind stirring the mural of the high desert.

Over the next few days, I thought often about the suggestion. I asked friends if they had heard of the idea of the Divine Mother, and while many had, no one was able to explain to me who She is. My curiosity intensified, and I became determined to unravel the mystery. I decided to pray to Her, yet my tone was detached, as if I was speaking to a phantom. "Divine Mother, I am praying to You now. Please help me on my journey." I offered little else, for I did not comprehend to whom I was speaking.

Days later, my life irrevocably shifted.

adventures of a
displaced princess

⌀

The Mother of All Things

As the sun kissed the Sangre de Christo mountains* early one morning, I settled into meditation and found beautiful guides in the etheric forming an arch above my head. I acknowledged their grace, and with a flair of arrogance, I heard myself announce, "I would like to speak with the Divine Mother!"

In a single instant, a flash of pink lightning came from the heavens, separated the arch of angels and anchored in my body. Every cell was filled with the intensity of this light. My physical body felt paralyzed and I did not dare to try to move. I was frozen with the brilliance of this energy, every part of me except my mind which could still produce thoughts.

My first thought was, "Oh my God, this is Her!"

There was no doubt that my request had been answered. The parting of the angels, the shade of pink and the intensity of the light could only be one Being. She had me completely enraptured in Her brilliance, and I felt a mixture of absolute awe and pure terror. As I wondered what one would say to the Divine Mother, She spoke first.

I will never forget Her words. In the tone a mother uses when she wants to be absolutely clear with her child, a tone of precision that struck me with terror, She said, "YOU ARE

* *The Sangre de Christo mountains grace northern New Mexico. The Spanish name translates to 'Blood of Christ'.*

NOTHING WITHOUT ME!"

My shock intensified, and all I could offer in response was a meek, "All right." I was certainly not going to argue with a force whose energy was clearly as vast as the universe, yet I was not able to enthusiastically agree.

My feeble response did not seem to satisfy Her, and She repeated, in the same ferocious tone, "YOU ARE **NOTHING** WITHOUT ME!" There was not a hint of leniency in Her voice, and although I did not comprehend Her words, I knew She would not waiver.

"All right," I said again, this time with more sincerity.

And so, my conscious work with the Mother began.

I do not remember all of the details of this first communion. The experience was so extraordinary that I assumed I would never forget a single word of it, and so I did not bother to write it down. I would simply repeat the conversation over and over again in my mind and bask in the memory. However, as time has passed and my connection with the Divine Mother has only grown in intensity and brilliance, what was once unforgettable has now become a part of my life.

I do remember the Mother answered a question that had been haunting me. Ever since it had been suggested that I commune with Her, I had wondered who She was. To me She was only a concept, but one that I honored enough to pray to.

Still using a tone that was unquestionable in authority, She said to me, "Everything you see is the Mother, everything you touch is the Mother, everything you feel is the Mother, everything you taste is the Mother, everything you hear is the Mother, everything you think is the Mother, everything you are is the Mother." These words remain the best definition of the Divine Mother I have ever received.

Some call Her the feminine face of God, others the Goddess. To me She is the Mother of All Things.

For my own assurance, I asked the guides of light that accompanied me on my journey if it was in my highest interest to align with this force. They expressed uniformly and unequivocally that they too report to Her, that Her light commands All, and each of us is simply a drop of water in Her wake.

At the end of the first session with the Mother, I asked Her what my work was to be on this planet. I expected Her to offer me a glorious assignment.

She simply said, "Tend to the earth."

I wondered what She meant, and I imagined that I would create a huge center focused on gardening. I had never even planted a small garden and had only once grown flowers, but I assumed my assignment would be vast.

I asked Her to be more specific.

She responded with an energy of pure love that seemed to rage, "My plant is thirsty!"

"Plant? What plant?" I wondered.

Then I remembered! Two days earlier, my housemate and I had hauled a large, flowering geranium out of the meditation room and onto the porch to create more space for morning yoga.

I looked outside and was horrified to see the glorious plant had been almost destroyed by the night wind of the high desert. Most of the brilliant red blossoms were gone, and the remaining branches hung over the side, completely flattened by the storm.

The pot was large and it had taken two people to pull it onto the porch. Without hesitation, I immediately lugged the ailing plant back indoors. I remembered the Mother's comment about thirst, and I thought to go to the kitchen for water.

"No!" She commanded, "Feed the plant from the stream!"

I took my oversized water cup and ran down the stairs, out the back door and over to the stream that ran through the property. I filled the cup, ran back to the house, up to the room and I fed the plant.

"More!" She ordered, and I followed instructions once again.

"More," She repeated, and so back to the stream I ran.

Three cups seemed to satiate the Mother, and I was offered a rest. As I sat down and leaned against the wall, I remember looking at the ailing plant and feeling horrified that almost nothing was left except for the roots and a few torn branches. I wondered if it would ever regain its outer brilliance.

Within a few weeks of the plant's return to shelter, it grew into a spectacular shade of green. In time, it was once again filled with red blossoms that were even more vibrant and plentiful than before.

It was only months later I would realize that my own path with the Mother would mirror that of the plant's. Time and time again I would feel abandoned in the midst of a storm. I would experience the outer layers of myself being ripped away, seemingly without mercy. I would watch my beliefs, ideas, image, and identity crumble with a single breath from the Mother of All Things. Many times, I would be dragged back to shelter to look at myself and wonder if I would ever again recover.

Hidden Grace

After my first encounter with the Divine Mother, I spent the following days enraptured in amazement. I was both thrilled and overwhelmed by the connection I had made. As spring continued to unfold and the stream began to fill with water from the melting snow, I wondered if the connection would be a once in a lifetime experience or if She would return. I prayed She would come to me again, and five days after our original communion, I had the courage to call on Her presence.

As I sat to formally meditate, I asked for the Mother. In the next instant, Her light engulfed my being and the brilliance of Divine love coursed through every cell of my body. This time, as I was consumed in Her blazing love, the Mother informed me that I needed training in following orders. Once again, Her words seemed odd. In that moment, I did not realize I would spend the next month in what would feel like an Army obedience course, but I did know that She had become a regular part of my life.

Before my communion with the Mother, I had been accustomed to moving through my day from a space of logic and a sense of false control. In my own mind, I was a master at managing tasks, and I prided myself in making sure everything was taken care of properly. I handled a job, pursued my path, kept an active social life and took care of my home. Yet, when the Mother's course in obedience began, it felt as though my life was slowly being pulled away from my own hands. She began to appear to me at random times throughout my day and give me very explicit instructions. I was regularly irritated by Her requests, and I would often rebel and sometimes even rage. Yet, in the end, I almost always followed. I knew what it was like to try to handle everything myself, and it too was treacherous. This new path scared me because I felt such a lack of control, but it also fascinated me. I was curious to see how the Mother of All Things would navigate the course of this young woman's life.

While my greatest passion was my pursuit of the Divine, and my connection to Her was a dream come true, fear still surfaced. I was not willing to surrender without a fight. With Her every suggestion, I felt the Mother was not seeing the whole picture, and only time and experience would prove to me that She IS the whole picture. As I continued down my path, I would eventually realize that Her intention was never to hurt or punish me in any way, but always to serve me.

The earlier requests were simple. One day I was driving in town, diligently following a prepared list of errands, and the Mother appeared in my mind's eye asking me to completely rearrange my list. It was a simple request, but it did not make sense. She asked that I immediately go to the natural spring for water, even before I went to the store at the other end of town to buy a second jug to carry more water.

I had been raised in a family of engineers and I was trained to question everything irrational. "No," I responded, "I will not go to the spring now, and then again later after I buy the second jug. I do not have time to waste. It will all be done at once." I was sure I knew how to handle the situation best, and I also remember thinking She obviously did not understand the inconvenience of running all over town.

The moment that thought left my mind, She responded. It was not with words, but with a flare of Her energy. A reddish-pink light erupted, filling the etheric world, and She did not need to speak. I was offered a glimpse of Her power and was reminded once again who She is. I instantly turned the car toward the spring.

As it turned out, the store at the other end of town was out of water jugs, and the Mother's plan was indeed the most efficient.

Another time She asked me to volunteer to clean my neighbor's house. I was horrified because cleaning is a chore I absolutely abhor. This particular neighbor had four large dogs who lived indoors and left trails of hair everywhere. The house was dark and dank, and it seemed it could never be cleaned.

Following orders, I went to the neighbor and told her I was to clean her house while she was to sit outside on a lounge chair in the sun. To my surprise, tears rolled down the woman's cheeks and she said, "I cannot do that." This woman had always presented herself as a pillar of strength, yet she actually began trembling. She who always handled everything was being asked to sit back, and her tears showed her terror.

Personally, I would have been happy to take her place in the lounge chair while she cleaned her own house, but the directions were explicit, and I had committed to following them. Her tears continued and she said, "I am not comfortable resting while another works. In fact, I rarely rest."

Then I understood it was the perfect assignment for both of us. I saw cleaning as undesirable and fruitless work, and she viewed resting as unworthy. We were both being asked to honor an aspect of life that was uncomfortable for us. Eventually, I persuaded her to sit in the lounge chair, and I began to clean. I wish I could say I spent every moment on this cleaning spree singing praise to the Divine, but I did not. I grumbled almost the entire time. It was a large house, and I was concerned I might have to clean the whole thing. Frightening visions of being asked to clean the entire house, every week for the rest of my life, passed through my mind. And when I really wanted to terrorize myself, I decided the Mother would ask me to clean houses as a profession.

Fortunately, the world of spirit had mercy on me. After I finished cleaning the kitchen, the beautiful neighbor stumbled into the house, and this time her body was really shaking. Her jaw trembled so intensely she could barely speak. Eventually, I was able to understand her words as she whispered, "The Mother came to me!" As she had relaxed in the lounge chair, she had been gifted with the grace of the Divine Mother's presence. In her own mind's eye, the Mother appeared to her and offered the promise of eternal love.

As my course in following orders continued, one day the Mother of All Things asked me to drink from the stream that ran through the property I lived on.

"No way!" I said, as my rebellious nature raged. Everyone in the village knew the stream was contaminated with giardia, and neighbors told horror stories of becoming very ill even from a small sip of the water. I was not willing to be sick, even for the Divine Mother.

"You will not become ill," She assured me, "Hold the water in your hands before you drink, and ask the light to purify it. Drink from the stream three times."

It took me a number of weeks to fulfill this request. I was both horrified and elated by the suggestion. I feared becoming very ill from the contaminated water, while I was excited by the possibility that She would protect me. As I debated the request, I found myself wondering if I had understood correctly. Yet, the suggestion had been very clear the moment it transpired, and not following would signify my consciously turning away from the Mother's call.

Then one afternoon, a flood of light poured through me after a communion with Her, and I knew it was time. I was so filled with Her love that nothing could have harmed me. I was in a space of complete grace. I walked to the stream, lay on the small bridge and leaned the front of my body over the water. Three times, without fear, I held the water in my hands, prayed over it and drank it.

It was completely freeing to do so. I had honored the Mother's request, and I had made another step toward releasing my illusions around logic, control and safety.

I never once had a hint of giardia in my body.

Another day at the Mother's suggestion, I drove four hours to visit a retreat center where I had lived the previous year. I was told I needed to clear some karma I had created during my stay as an employee. The clearing happened within the first two hours of my stay.

Soon afterward, the sun began to set, and I heard Her say, "You can go now."

I was not in the mood to drive another four hours that night. "I would like to stay a bit," I responded.

"All right," She offered, "but do not stay long."

That night, I slept beneath the stars, and the next morning, a friend of mine at the center offered to give me a massage. I was thrilled. I had learned the art of massage when I had lived there, and since I had communed with the Mother I had been giving other people massages at Her request, but I had not received one myself in quite some time. The last weeks with the Mother had been glorious and demanding. I was both graced by Her brilliance and challenged by Her requests. My body was tired.

Just before I was to receive the gift, the Mother came to me and said, "Do not stay for the massage. Leave the property now."

A flash of fury passed through me. Suddenly, I felt I had been bossed around by this Being for weeks. I had been a slave to another's will, I had done my best to follow, and now all I wanted was to lie on a massage table and receive. I protested, "I am down here in a body, and my body wants a massage! I need this for me. I will do work for You later."

At that moment, I could feel a descension of angels and other beautiful beings all around me. Their message was the same, "Please, do not stay for the massage."

I felt ganged up on, and I retorted, "I am the only one in a body. You are all floating in bliss and you don't understand the pain of being in the physical. I do. And I am staying for this massage!"

Their attempts at persuading me did not cease, nor did my stand.

Finally, I said, "Listen. I'm asking for your help. I know I have been told not to stay, and I know I am going against the Mother's will by receiving the massage. It is wrong, but I am choosing to do it, so please help me. Whatever it is that is needed, please give it to me."

Finally, it came time to lay on the massage table. "Thank

God," I thought, "I made it!"

I settled my body onto the table expecting to find comfort. The moment I shut my eyes, the Mother appeared before me in all of Her radiance and said in a tone of steel, "Get *off* the table!"

"I will not get off the table," I responded, "So please help me. You are the Mother of All Things, so you can surely help. Please just give me this massage." I was determined to stay, and I felt sure the world of spirit could prevent whatever it was the Mother and angels were so concerned about.

Moments later, the massage began and I immediately understood their concern. The energy of my friend was very dense. I could see and feel and even taste that the force coming through his hands and filling my body was dark. It felt as though a heavy substance was being fed into my cells. I was horrified and I cried to the Mother, "Please help me! Please channel Your energy through him so this darkness will not be fed into me."

She responded gently, "He is too dense and he cannot receive My pure energy. This is why I asked you not to stay for the massage. Your energy has become much lighter since you left here almost a year ago. You do not realize how much you have transformed. This center as a whole vibrates at a much lower frequency than you do now. There is a lot of energy here which pulls you down. That is why you must go. One day, you will be strong enough to retain your true frequency even in the midst of the darkest of darkness, but now you are not."

I struggled with the truth of the situation and with the desire not to hurt my friend by getting off of the table only moments after the massage had begun. I wanted desperately to leave, but in the end I did not have the inner strength and confidence to stand in my higher truth. I chose to stay, yet I cried inside.

When the massage was finally over, I raised my body, which felt contaminated with darkness, and I made a straight line for my car. I spent the next four hours driving home, tears flowing from my eyes almost the entire way. My body ached from the darkness that was infused into it, and my heart was breaking. I was deeply sad that the Mother and beautiful beings of light had tried so desperately to help me and I had walked the other way. I had said I wanted to follow the light of truth, and I had sworn my life to spirit, but when they had made a simple request, I had chosen not to follow.

It was powerful for me to realize that the Mother's intention, which was clothed in strictness, was only to serve me. It was not Herself She was honoring, but me. I realized on the long drive that my statement about doing something for myself in one moment and something for Her in another was ludicrous. It was always for me.

I arrived home very late that night and crawled into bed. The next morning, I was still deeply sad. I sat in meditation and prayed to the Mother.

"I am sorry," I cried, "I realize You were only trying to help me, and I turned away from You. I really want to serve You. I really want to follow. Please forgive me."

In complete graciousness, She offered, "You were forgiven the moment the incident occurred. Simply start again."

"How brilliant," I thought. The slate was instantly wiped clean. The past was the past, and in that moment, I could start fresh.

"Anything, Mother! I will do anything you ask!"

And so we began again.

Escaping Illusion

As the weeks passed, I was lured into discovering the benefits of following the Mother's command and the requests became more outrageous. My life already had elements that others considered shocking. I had lived in five states within the last six years, and my external life seemed to be in constant flux. I found new work and living situations through my meditations, and the only consistent pattern I could boast was my loyalty to my guidance.

While my material life was unstable, I always had my safety nets. At the time the Divine Mother came to me, I had a strong savings, I had insurance for my health and my car, and I had a job as the marketing and publicity director for a book publishing company. Also my family was wealthy, and I knew I could turn to them if I needed help.

In a matter of a few weeks, all of my safety nets were gone. I had nothing, except my conscious connection to Her.

The guidance to surrender it all did not come at once. It came in steps that seemed to get closer together as time passed. I do not remember the order of the Mother's commands to relinquish all that I held onto so tightly, only that with each suggestion, I felt terror. I fought and screamed and demanded the Mother take back Her requests. It was ludicrous for someone like me who did not lead a materially stable life to give away all that kept her safe.

When I explained this to the Mother, She only had one response, "It is *I* who keep you safe, nothing else."

She would not argue with me, or flatter my tirades, and She never wavered. I felt absolutely trapped. I would never forgive myself if I did not have the courage to follow the Mother of All Things, and I was petrified to live without my safety nets.

Yet, with each request, I eventually submitted. The moment one request was fulfilled I expected a period of rest, but in the next moment, She would ask me to give up one more thing. So within three weeks, I gave away all of my savings except two thousand dollars (also Her request), I canceled all forms of insurance, and I left my job. I also left the security of knowing I could turn to my family for help. They were atheists and they openly disapproved of my passion for the spiritual. Turning to them, in light of what I had done, would have meant a complete defeat of all that I believed in.

Well, I still had $2,000, and that was plenty for basic survival, at least for a time. I was grateful the Mother left me with a cushion.

Then, it happened...

Living Grace

Just after I had relinquished most of my material security, the Divine Mother appeared to me for the first time in the form of a woman who exists on the earth plane. I was meditating peacefully when a brilliant, elderly Indian woman appeared to my left side. I immediately recognized Her as one of the living incarnations of the Divine Mother a dear friend had told me about.

Three years earlier I had spent a summer living in a Yoga Ashram and befriended a young, bohemian woman named Carla. Contrary to my atheist upbringing, Carla was raised by her spiritually flamboyant father, and they often traveled to far off places to be with various spiritual teachers. They were regularly enchanted with one guru or another, and their devotion to any particular form seemed to sway as easily as a willow in the wind.

In the months before the Divine Mother appeared to me, I repeatedly saw a single image in my meditations. A round, purple dot occasionally appeared right before my mind's eye and then moved away and disappeared into the distance. The pattern would repeat itself over and over again. One evening, I mentioned it to Carla.

"Oh my God!" she declared. "I saw the same purple dot

every time Amma* touched my head!"

"Amma?" I asked, thoroughly confused.

"The Indian woman who is a living incarnation of the Divine
Mother. I visited Her at Her home in Italy. Do you remember?"

"The one who lives in a mountain village with Her sister and
Her sister's Italian husband?" I responded as I remembered that
"Amma" means "Mother" in the ancient Indian language of
Sanskrit.

"Yes! That's the one!" she beamed, "She is for you! I am sure
of it because every time I was with Her, I thought of you."

I was skeptical. At the time, I did not desire to follow a
spiritual teacher. The thought of being told how to commune
with God made my rebellious nature rage. Carla could feel my
reserve.

"She is an Avatar. She was born as an incarnation of the
Divine Mother to help all of us. She does not have an ashram or
formal followers, and there are no rules surrounding Her. She
does not even speak to those who come to sit with Her. She
simply transmits Divine light to help people open further to
God."

"I don't think it would be my scene," I stated honestly.

"There's no scene around Her!" Carla declared, "Very few
people know she exists. She has never granted an interview or
allowed Her picture to be published. She says She calls the
individuals to Her when the time is right, and there is no reason
for Her to be known to the world.

"You'll love Her," she promised sweetly as she began to dig
through a seemingly endless stack of spiritual books and pictures

* *'Amma ' is not the actual name of this incarnation of the Divine Mother. While
She blessed the writing of this story, She asked to remain anonymous.*

that decorated her floor.

"Here She is!" she said triumphantly, handing me a blurred photograph of the face of an elderly Indian woman.

The entire picture seemed to be out of focus, except for Her two eyes which offered a gaze that was so brilliant it sent a chill down my spine. I was speechless as Her light seemed to enter the deepest part of my being. "I would like to visit Her someday," I thought to myself as I returned the picture to Carla.

Now, months later, as I sat in meditation, the woman I had once admired in a photograph stood next to me on the etheric plane. She did not appear with fanfare, only with the brilliance of God's light. As I acknowledged Her presence, She said very simply, "Come to Me."

"Aren't You here with me now?" I responded.

"Yes, and come to Me in Italy." Her words were direct and concise.

"Shall I come in August?" I asked randomly. We were in the first part of May.

"No, earlier," She stated.

"Late June?"

"Earlier."

"Early June?"

"Go to the wedding and then come to Me," She suggested.

"Wedding?" I pondered, "What wedding?"

Instantly, I remembered I had been invited to a wedding in Sicily, the southern part of Italy, by a young woman I had met two years earlier when she had spent a summer living in the United States. I had received the invitation weeks earlier, and I did not even consider attending. Now, I definitely would.

Slightly trembling, I arose from the meditation to look for the wedding invitation. I found it buried under a stack of papers and old mail. I opened the cream colored card embossed with an image of Mount Etna, the volcano on the island of Sicily, to read that the ceremony would be held on June eleventh. "The vision must have been real," I assured myself.

I soon began making travel arrangements, and I wrote to my Sicilian friend to let her know I would attend her celebration. Suddenly, I realized the cushion of $2,000 the Mother had left me was almost completely depleted by the simple words, "Come to Me."

Down to Nothing

Since the requests to relinquish all of my material safety nets had come in steps, I did not realize the full extent of the plan until it had already been acted upon. It was only when I had given away everything that it struck me.

"My God!" I thought, "I have NOTHING!"

Suddenly, I felt horrified by the end result of my many steps. I entered into meditation, sobbing hysterically. My whole body trembled, and all I could say over and over again was, "Mother! I am giving up EVERYTHING for you! EVERYTHING!"

Then She appeared to me in a mist of pink light. In a ferocious roar that ironically filled my body with peace, She raged, "You are giving up NOTHING!"

Instantly, the truth of Her words pierced my heart and the bliss of the Divine showered my being. It was true, and deep down I knew it. I had given away nothing, except the illusion of security.

During the month between the time I purchased the ticket and the time I left for Amma's, I vacillated between elation and despair. I felt the thrill of throwing everything to the wind and trusting the world of spirit would provide for me, as well as the torment of the possibility that it would not.

My greatest fear was that I would discover that the world of spirit was not real. There was a chance I would learn through my actions that the Divine was only a figment of my imagination, something I had created to make my life have more meaning. Possibly, it was all a fantasy.

In moments of fear, I was tormented with visions of being destitute for the rest of my life. I might become like the poor crop workers I had read about in school, the ones who never got out of debt and were kept as virtual slaves.

I also feared that the advice of spirit was not appropriate for the material plane. Maybe the heavens and earth existed as two totally separate worlds that could never come together, even though my deepest prayer was that they would.

Conversely, in the moments of communing with the Divine Mother, every part of my being knew She was real and that Her love for me was as vast as the universe. Even when Her words or suggestions terrified me, I always felt completely safe in Her presence and I knew I was absolutely cared for.

It was in the moments I did not feel Her conscious presence that I felt true terror. One morning, as I stumbled through the kitchen trying to prepare breakfast, I felt the grip of fear tighten around my neck. My energy became frantic and I knew I needed to connect with the Divine or fear would quickly consume me. I did not feel capable of communing with the Mother in meditation, so I walked outside to connect with Her physical presence.

There were still hints of late winter in the air and I was appropriately layered in two shirts, long pants, a gortex jacket and gloves. I felt instantly soothed by the kiss of nature, and I wanted more of the same. Patches of snow graced the landscape, yet I took off my boots and began walking in my bare feet on the dirt road in front of the house. As I walked and prayed, I spontaneously took off my gloves and reached down to pick up a handful of mud. The wet earth felt heavenly, and I began massaging it into my hands. The mud radiated the Mother's bliss and I longed to be absorbed in Her brilliance. When my hands were thoroughly consumed by Her touch, I suddenly began spreading Her light over my face. The sensation of the Mother cradling my face was so soothing that the mud soon found its way into my hair and down my neck.

Before I knew it, the layers of clothing were gradually being left on the side of the road, as I covered my entire body in mud. I yearned only to be drenched in Her love and when I came to a mud puddle near the side of the road, I sat down in bliss. My clothes rested on a rock beside the puddle and my naked body basked in the reverence of the Divine. As I covered every inch of me in Her grace, I felt the same communion I had known in my meditations coursing through my body. I was bathed in feminine power, and the force of the Goddess had engulfed my being.

My peace was broken only by the faint sound of a motor in the distance. As I returned from my altered state, I noticed a pickup truck approaching. I quickly grabbed my clothes and carried my mud-covered body low into the world of sage brush and cedar trees. As I sprinted through the wilderness, completely naked and covered in earth, I felt myself align with Her rhythm. I wove instinctively between the trees and over the rugged terrain with a perfect connection to the Being from whom I had emerged. As I navigated my body with grace and ease, in an instant, I was no longer a woman. I had become a deer gliding through the woods.

After the truck had passed, I offered my deep gratitude to the Mother, and I gradually layered my clothes over my mud skin. As I walked home, I knew from that moment on, that in the midst of terror, I could lie naked on the earth and the fear that seemed to be engulfing my being would simply flow out of my body. The gift of being held directly by Her makes all fear instantly lose its facade of power, because all that is not truth disintegrates in the pure presence of the Divine.

Occasionally, I forgot this simple truth. After I had given away what seemed to be everything yet appeared to Her to be nothing, I knew the false sense of control I had held onto for so long was slipping through my fingers. The life I had so fervently tried to order seemed no longer to be mine.

At times the sense of loss and confusion was overwhelming. My life was clearly being ruled by a force much greater than myself, and I never knew what the next instant might bring. Everything seemed to be out of hand. All I had was a plane ticket to visit an incarnation of the Divine Mother and little else. Was I to work? Or to suffer? Or to sit still and trust? I did not know.

I took a walk near my home one morning and realized I had no idea what to do. Rather than gently ask the Mother for direction in my meditation, I stormed up and down the dirt road near my home, screaming, "You tell me, Mother! You tell me, because I don't know!" I yelled and screamed until I exhausted myself with my own tirade, and then I realized the truth in my fury. I needed the Divine to guide me.

Another day, I drove down a dirt road on my way to town pondering the Mother's most recent words that She may ask me to give up my car. "Forget it!" I decided internally, "I will not sell this car because that definitely does not make sense." The car had so many miles on it that it was not worth a cent according to the resale book, yet it ran perfectly. It would be almost impossible for me to be able to buy a better car for what that one was worth. Plus, my car was pretty. It had leather seats, a full stereo, and it only looked to be a few years old.

As those thoughts passed through my mind the Mother appeared to me, and said very simply, "If there is a moment in time when I ask you to release the car and you do not, I will blow it up!"

I was stunned! The message was very clear. Limited human beliefs do not rule this plane. She does. She is in charge, and the only path that truly makes sense is to follow Her command.

As I sat in the wake of this experience, it was clear I had come too far to turn back. At the same time, it was far too painful to stand still. My only choice was to go forward.

A few days before I left for Europe, I visited a friend of mine. I told him I thought I might be in trouble. I explained I had given away everything as a result of following the messages I received in my meditations, and now I only had a plane ticket to Europe.

I will always be grateful for his response because it offered me the courage I needed to continue forth. After my detailed description of everything that had occurred, the first thing he said was, "You are so lucky!" Then, he continued, "I would give anything to have guidance as clear as yours. Many people would. You are so fortunate because each step is handed to you."

"But don't you think I blew it? Do you really think that was guidance?" I asked.

"It makes perfect sense to me," he said, "You are going to the Divine Mother, and She has asked that you come to Her naked. It is a birth for you, and every child comes into the world completely naked."

Less than twenty-four hours before I left on my trip, my housemate became furious at my refusal to deliver her love letters to my good friend's husband, and she asked me to move out of the beautiful home we had been sharing. I packed all afternoon and evening. Long after dark, I moved my belongings into my neighbor's spare bedroom. Then at two o'clock in the morning, when the last load had been delivered, my car battery exploded.

As the sun rose from behind the mountains, I traveled the first piece of my three hour journey to the airport in a tow truck, wondering if I would ever make it to the plane. The burly driver offered sweet words of comfort as I cried in gratitude, fear, excitement and trepidation.

The car was quickly repaired in the nearby town, and I continued to the airport. My first thought as I settled into the small seat that would carry me across the ocean was, "Thank God! I made it!"

That was before I realized the journey had only begun.

The Sweet Life

The wedding in Italy was an extravagant affair, and it was a wonderful way to arrive in a foreign land. I flew into Catania, a city on the eastern shore of Sicily, and was met by the brother and sister of the bride. They immediately ushered me to the family country home surrounded by fields of fruit trees. I spent two days before the wedding under the watchful and loving eye of my friend's grandmother as I helped to prepare the extraordinary feast of Sicilian delights.

Most of her family and friends spoke very little English, but I had studied Italian as a University student. My mother was Italian, and for that reason I believe I learned the language quite easily. I had lived in Italy for a semester in college and had visited the country on a number of occasions. For me, it was a second home and a place where I felt very safe and very loved.

In Sicily, the native dialect was usually spoken, and it was one I could not understand. While most of the younger people also knew proper Italian, many of the elders did not. The grandmother regularly laughed at the expressions on my face as I tried to decipher her words.

The wedding was held in an exquisite church that hosted the most beautiful and simple crucifix I had ever seen. Great pillars offered strength throughout the cross-shaped structure and carvings of saints' faces lined the ceiling.

The evening reception was held outdoors with the back drop

of an amazing sunset and then a blanket of stars. I was the only guest from a foreign country, and I felt incredibly welcomed throughout the entire celebration. At the end of the evening, many of the guests had left and only a group of younger ones remained. I was very touched when a playful declaration was made that only proper Italian, rather than the local dialect, be spoken in my honor. Then, two of the groom's friends pretended to be bartenders while they told jokes and even sang songs in English.

After the day of celebration, I spent the remainder of the week traveling in Sicily, staying with people I had met at the wedding. I was grateful for the extraordinary hospitality which offered a soft and pleasant reprieve from my last few months in the United States.

Soon enough, it was time to venture north to the region of Tuscany to a small village that rested in a saddle of the mountains.

Holy Hosts

I traveled by train to the city of Prato, then a local bus carried me into the Monti di Calvana, the beautiful mountains that rest north of Florence. As the bus climbed through an array of switchbacks, we passed a number of small villages before reaching the one that held the blessing of a living incarnation of the Divine Mother.

Once in Amma's village, the bus driver signaled that we were arriving at my stop. As I walked to the front of the bus, I asked the driver to direct me toward the campground where I had made reservations to stay.

In a matter of moments, the locals on the bus were in a flurry. They chatted frantically among themselves and then communicated to me that there was no camping available in the area.

"I must camp," I responded, knowing I did not have enough money to stay in a hotel for eight nights.

The bus continued to roll along, and I had to make a decision or I would find myself back in Prato. I mentioned Amma's name, and my beautiful companions seemed to relax. Two women invited me to exit the bus with them.

One of the women reiterated there was no camping in the area, but I could come with her. She knew Amma and we would go to Her home together and ask what to do.

As we walked, she told me the story of Amma coming to

Italy many years earlier as a teenager. Her older sister had been living in the saddle village with her Italian husband and their two children. One winter, Amma's niece became very ill, and the doctors could not diagnose the problem or find the cure. The girl was too sick to travel, and so Amma came to her. The Mother of All Things held the small child for days and sang to her of the deities in heaven. Each day the child's health improved, and soon she was strong and healthy once again.

Meanwhile, Amma fell in love with the power of the mountains, the vastness of the views and the charm of the village. She decided to stay and make it Her home. She now lives on the small estate Her sister's husband inherited.

As we approached Amma's home, I could tell the other woman was offering me a gift, yet she spoke in a strong dialect and I could not understand her words. The first woman translated it into proper Italian, and I realized Isabella was a neighbor of Amma and she was inviting me to stay in her house. She said I could sleep in a room or camp in her yard, whichever I chose.

I was thrilled, and I accepted immediately.

Within a few minutes, we arrived at Isabella's home and I was ushered inside. Seven curious children piled down the stairs to meet me. As introductions were made, I realized Isabella was a single mother of four kids, and their house was the favorite hangout of the neighborhood children. Only the mother and the oldest girl spoke a tiny bit of proper Italian, so we mainly communicated through sign language and smiles.

There was an instant bond of love between us, and the entire group took me upstairs to see the rooms I could stay in if I chose. The house was three stories high. Pieces of the staircase banister were missing, a chunk of the wall had fallen out and everything was in a state of disrepair. I absolutely loved it.

I chose one of the abandoned rooms to stay in, and I set down all of my belongings. Then I followed the mother and the two youngest children downstairs to the kitchen. I had brought an enormous amount of food from the grocery store in Prato, and I displayed all of the treasures on the kitchen table. Isabella and the children knew I was communicating that the food was for all of us and I was suggesting an evening feast.

The little ones were thrilled until they looked at the contents of the food. Then they sadly turned to me and asked, "Vegetariana?"

"Sí," I responded, realizing how disappointing the contents would be to most children. It was all health food and there were no signs of meat, dairy or sugar.

Then the boy began flinging open the refrigerator and cabinets to display an impressive array of processed, packaged, sugar food. He explained that even the kids in the family smoked and drank, and they were not very interested in health. I explained I practiced yoga and meditation every day, and I never smoked and rarely drank. This made us laugh hysterically. We came from two seemingly different worlds and fell in love within a moment's time.

The laughter and joy were interrupted by a petrifying thought that crossed through my mind. Absolutely everything I had brought with me, except for the food, was upstairs with five teenagers. The little money I had, my passport, plane ticket, camping gear, EVERYTHING!

I tried to act casual, but I bolted up two flights of stairs to check on my belongings. I ran to the room I had chosen and when I looked inside, it took all of my strength to prevent tears from rolling down my face.

A sensation of love poured through me as I watched the three teenage boys busy at work. One had carried in a mattress and was preparing a sleeping space, another was repairing a light fixture so I would have a reading lamp near the bed, and the third was sweeping the floor. It was the most beautiful gift I had received in a week filled with generosity. Moments later, the two teenage girls arrived and they had in their hands more gifts. They offered me small bottles of shampoo, lotion and even perfume for my stay. It was absolutely precious, and I felt flooded with gratitude for such grace.

Amma's Light

In the early evening, the family sat with me while I ate my dinner, and we laughed almost the entire time. Then Alexandro, the young boy of eleven, walked me to the nearby chapel, and I felt elated with the expectation of seeing the beautiful Mother for the first time.

A group of visitors had already formed in front of the humble structure. I immediately noticed that most of them were middle-aged and they looked much more sophisticated than I in my short summer dress.

Soon, the chapel door swung open, and a small man stood before us with a clipboard of authority.

"Buona sera. Good evening," he beamed to the group in a heavy French accent, "Welcome to Amma's. My name is Francois, and I will check you in this evening. Please leave your shoes in the entrance way before you enter the chapel, and once inside you may choose any seat that is not already taken."

Amidst a scurry of shoes flying off feet, he turned to me since I was nearby and asked with less enthusiasm, "What is your name?"

"Walker," I responded.

He looked calmly at first and then frantically through the computer printout which clearly offered the names of those who had reservations for the Mother's darshan that evening.

"Your name is not here! You do not have reservations," He

said coldly. "You must wait on the side until everyone else has been seated, and if there is room, you will be able to enter."

I felt my heart sink, and my ecstasy instantly melted into despair. How could my name not be on the list?! I had definitely made reservations for eight evenings of darshan. I clearly remembered the friendly Indian woman's voice when I had called Amma's home a month earlier. "Yes, you can come those two weekends," she had offered. And even beyond reservations, my schedule had been dictated by the Mother herself. How could there be any confusion?

I stood to the side just behind Francois, fearing there may not be room once everyone else had entered.

Then I had an idea. I knew if my name was written on his papers, I could find it since I was accustomed to looking for my own name on lists. Fortunately, Francois was short, and I quietly stood on my toes and peered over his right shoulder. I prayed my presence would go unnoticed, and in all of the commotion, he did not realize that my eyes were ferociously scanning the list he held. In moments, I spotted my name.

"There it is!" I yelled in my excitement which clearly startled him. "That's my name, right there! Susan Walker!" It was handwritten at the end of an alphabetical computer print out.

"You must have made your reservation late!" Francois scowled. He did not share in my excitement. "You may enter," he offered without a hint of a smile.

I bolted in, set my shoes down with the others and went straight to the big chair before the altar where the Mother would sit. I glanced at the pews nearest to Her chair and for a few moments I pondered intensely over which seat to choose. I decided on one that was just in front and to the right of where the Mother would rest her gaze. An Indian woman standing nearby smiled at me as I put my sweater on the bench. "That will be a fine seat," she offered with assurance and laughter.

Soon the small chapel was packed with visitors and the air of expectation.

When it was time for the Mother to enter, we all rose to welcome Her. With my hands in prayer, I gratefully acknowledged the delicate, Indian woman who appeared at the side door. My very first thought as I looked upon Her luminous form was, "That's Her! That's the woman who came to me in my meditation!" I was elated to know I had come to the perfect place.

Amma's head was lowered, and without fanfare or arrogance, She walked to the front of the chapel. She wore a brilliant golden sari laced with silver embroidery that was dulled only by the light that radiated from Her. Once She seated herself in the simple white chair, we all took our seats.

Then, one at a time, in no particular order, visitors moved toward the front of the chapel to kneel before the Mother. Spiritual teachers from India often transmit Divine light to their visitors through a ceremony such as this. It is known as darshan, and each darshan is unique to each teacher.

With Amma, as an individual knelt down, She would scoop his or her head onto Her lap and gently place Her hands on the back of the person's neck. Then She would make slow sweeping movements from the back of the neck to the crown of the head. After a matter of moments, She would lift the individual's head with Her hands and stare into the visitor's eyes. When She gently released Her hands from the person's head, it was the guest's cue to return to his or her seat.

As I observed this process, I realized I was looking upon the pure light of God in the form of a simple, Indian woman. Her form was beautiful, but not unique in itself. The magic was in the light that poured through the form. As She graced each guest with Her touch and Her gaze, Her body rocked consistently and subtly as though it was keeping time with the heartbeat of God.

The ceremony continued, and eventually I chose to kneel before the Mother. I trembled slightly as I raised my body and approached Her chair. I wondered if I would receive a powerful vision or a glance into a world I had not yet visited.

As I bowed before Her and She swept my head onto Her lap, I was surprised by the firmness of Her grasp. As Her hands rested on my neck and then began to stroke my head, I was only aware of my thoughts. They were simple. I was struck by Her fragrance and by the feeling of Her sari brushing my face. I remember thinking, "This is it! She's touching me," followed by fearful thoughts that I would not carry out the simple procedure correctly. No visions came.

As I felt Her hands grasp the sides of my head, I looked up to receive Her gaze. The first moment I looked into Her eyes, I did not see human eyes looking back, I saw the entire universe before me. I saw galaxies floating through all time and all space. The earth was simply a moment in this scene that represented a vastness beyond my comprehension.

Within moments, my consciousness re-focused on the deep brown eyes before me. They were staring at me intently, as though they were inviting every aspect of my being to come into the light.

My only thought was a simple, "Thank you."

In moments She released Her hands. I bowed my head, stood up and returned to my seat.

Darshan continued as I vacillated between being completely

entranced by Amma's physical presence and completely restless from sitting still for so long. At times, my eyes wandered around the chapel or my body gently swayed from side to side as it often does in formal meditation.

Any movement at all, I soon realized, was noticed and frowned upon by the Indian woman who had sweetly teased me about my contemplation over the perfect seat. I later learned Her name is Jyoti which means "light" in Sanskrit. She is Amma's sister, and she stood on the side of the chapel in her own array of brilliance during the ceremony. She seemed to have the role of the school marm, in charge of keeping the little ones in line.

When each person had received Her touch, Amma sat quietly for a few moments, and then rose to leave. All of us stood as She left the chapel as humbly and simply as She had entered.

Once She departed, the rest of us gradually began to move from our seats and share with one another our feelings and appreciation for the gift of being in Her physical presence. It was an odd sensation to know I had just experienced the inexplicable. I had been blessed beyond my comprehension by a person who radiated the vastness of God.

We eventually wandered into the entrance of the chapel where I had my second encounter with Francois. He was clearly in charge, and he looked at me with a scowl and immediately asked, "Where are your shoes?"

"I don't know," I answered honestly as I casually began to glance through the array of shoes decorating the entrance.

"Are these them? Are they over here?" he questioned absurdly.

"No," I responded, "I don't know where they are. I'm still looking."

"You must find them NOW!" he declared with fury, "We must lock the chapel."

"What about all of the others standing here who have not yet found their shoes?" I asked, with the arrogance of one who is happy to point out the rude nature of another.

"We cannot wait for you," he claimed.

I took my time anyway, and eventually found my simple, black flats.

Even with the two rounds with Francois, I was still elated, and I happily wandered to my hosts' home. I greeted my foster family and communicated that the darshan was exquisite and I was tired. The mother, Isabella, lovingly pointed me to my room. I fell fast asleep, completely engrossed in bliss, with the simple mantra, "Thank you, Mother," floating through my mind and heart.

The Dark Waters

I slept beautifully, yet the next morning, I still felt tired. Being in the presence of extraordinary light was demanding on my body. Just as I returned from the dream state, two of the children came to my room and insisted on taking me to a nearby pond to swim. The evening before they had asked me what I missed from home, and I had said I missed swimming. So off we went.

The pond was only a short walk from the Mother's home. It was sheltered and hidden by beautiful trees that were full with summer leaves. The oasis was cool, and the dirt bottom and plant life created a density and a sense of mystery to the water's brilliance. I was timid about swimming in such a mysterious pond. It was completely different than the chlorinated, carefully manicured swimming pools I was used to from home.

The pond's water was almost impossible to see through. Fortunately, I had my swimming goggles, so I could at least make out the dark figures of plant life that emerged from the pond's depth before I found myself entangled in their arms. Unlike the long, relaxing swims I was accustomed to in swimming pools, I found myself tense and irritated as a result of my insistence that nothing touch me unexpectedly. I moved slowly through the water, horrified each time something moved against my body. The only things I could see in the density below were simple fish and beautiful forms of seaweed, but they terrified me.

Alexandro, my young companion, seemed completely comfortable with all that swam with us in the pond. He laughed joyfully every time his face emerged from the water, and he seemed to treasure the warm caress of the plant life.

To try and lessen my terror, I decided to simply dive in, and I turned a somersault into the water. While doing so, my goggles slipped off of my head, and as I frantically searched for them in the darkness below, I knew I would never see them again. Now I had absolutely no hope of seeing all that lay before me in the darkness of the Mother.

It is only in hindsight that I understand the symbolic nature of that swim.

When we returned to the house, I lay my tired body in a bath. I was grateful for the warm, clean water and the chance to be completely still.

Suddenly there was a clatter through the house that sounded like an alarm. "Susan! Susan! Viéni! Viéni! (Come! Come!)" It was the flamboyant Alexandro yelling at me to get out of the bath. I did not smell smoke, nor did I hear sirens, and the water felt so blissful I decided to stay in. He and I would have plenty of time to play later.

A few moments passed, and Alexandro's voice echoed through the house once again. This time, I pulled myself out of the tub and hoped the commotion was worth leaving the comfort of the bath.

It was. I found Amma's sister, Jyoti, at the door waiting for me. She greeted me politely and said a few simple words that led my heart to crumble. "Mother has asked that you leave the neighbors' house. You must stay elsewhere."

Tears immediately filled my eyes. I could not believe what I was hearing.

"You must go," she reiterated, "Mother has said so."

A wave of sadness passed through me. In a short time, the neighbors had become my dear friends, and the thought of leaving the comfort of their home was frightening.

"Why must I go?" I asked.

"Mother has said so," she repeated, as though there were no more questions to be asked. But I had many questions. Disbelief and then anger raged through me. Why would the Mother of All Things need to ask a young woman not to stay with a neighbor? Why would She care? Why would She even notice? It must not be the Mother who wants me to go, I quickly decided, it must be her staff that has made the decision, and they are only saying it is the Mother's request.

Jyoti must have read my thoughts. She explained, "Mother asks that visitors do not stay with neighbors. Everyone must stay outside of the village."

"I didn't know that," I honestly responded. "I will go," I continued, "Although I'm a little scared. I'm not sure where I will stay. I would really like to camp."

"Oh no!" Jyoti laughed, "Do not camp. Stay in a hotel. I will give you a list of local pensions and you can call them to see who has space."

I told her I really wanted to camp and again she insisted on a hotel.

I conceded.

Then she asked me, "Why did you come to Mother? Were you backpacking through Italy and you decided to stop by?"

"No," I responded, "I came to Europe specifically to see Amma."

"Really?" she asked, as if it was a total surprise I consciously came to the Mother rather than accidentally stumbling upon Her.

Then I explained, "I receive regular guidance in my meditations, and recently Amma appeared to me and asked me to come to Her. I don't know very much about Her, only that I was to come."

"Oh, no," Jyoti offered with a gentle laugh, "Mother says one should not follow such guidance. She says when one sees Her in meditation, it is probably not even Her."

If I was meant to die from shock in this lifetime, it would have been at that moment.

"What?!" I demanded in return.

"You should not follow the guidance you receive in meditation, it is probably not true," she said with the casualness of one who is discussing the abhorrently mundane.

I had spent three years following the guidance I received in meditation. I had just given away every material security because of this guidance! I was standing in a tiny town in Italy without enough money for the rest of my trip because I acted on the messages I received in meditation! How could She say I was not to follow?!

I had nothing left to say to Jyoti.

I did my best to smile before I turned and walked back into the house. I went straight to my room, threw myself on the bed and cried. My entire body trembled and the sobs came from a depth which I had not before known.

"I was wrong," I thought, "She is not the Divine Mother. How could She be?" Suddenly, Amma seemed to be like so many of the teachers I had avoided on my path. The ones who had rules, regulations and restrictions, rather than the simple conveyance of Divine light. As tears streamed down my face, my heart seemed to ache with the pain from lifetimes of trying to rediscover the Divine, only to be disappointed along the way. Here I was, lying on a bed in Italy, having given away everything for the Mother of All Things, only to discover that Amma was not for me.

I sobbed deeply for at least an hour, and then I heard the familiar alarm of Alexandro's voice, "Susan! Susan! Viéni! Viéni! (Come! Come!)" This time, I was sure I would not respond to his call. I was lying in a fire of torment, paralyzed by pain.

Yet, his alarm continued, and eventually he came to the room. "Oh!" he said, surprised to see me in a sea of tears. Then he shrugged his shoulders and very gently and sweetly said, "Viéni. (Come.)" I could not resist the soft plea in his eyes and I raised myself off the bed. Taking my hand, he led me down the two flights of stairs, and I was able to stop the flow of tears just as he and I stepped out the front door. We walked only a few steps, and I found myself eye to eye with Francois.

"What are you doing staying at the neighbors'?!" he barked.

"I didn't know I wasn't supposed to stay there," I responded honestly.

"Well you cannot stay!" he seemed to yell, and the tears I had so ardently tried to suppress began to rise. "Don't get all emotional. That is ridiculous!" he ordered. His words seemed to crumble an invisible dam, and my tears began to flow with great passion.

"Why are you getting emotional?!" he demanded to know, "You simply must leave. Why did you go there in the first place? That was very disrespectful."

"I was looking for the campground," I began to explain through my tears, "and everyone said it didn't exist. Then Isabella invited me to stay at her home. We have all been very happy together. I like staying with them."

I imagine at that moment, Francois had an opportunity to display compassion, but he did not choose to do so. He became furious. As though a great battle had begun, he declared, "If you stay there tonight, you cannot come to darshan this evening!"

In that instant, I could have chosen to show restraint, but I did not. Even though I was sobbing, I did my best to yell back, "Then I will have to think about it!"

I could feel a sense of absolute disdain radiating from Francois, and I was not sure to whom it was directed. Then it crossed my mind that possibly he was in judgment of my new friends. They were a poor family with little education and no interest in the spiritual path.

"Listen!" I yelled as the sea of tears parted to honor my rage, "This family may drink, smoke, eat processed food, be overweight and never meditate, but they are loving! They welcomed a complete stranger into their home with love. As I evolve, I pray to be more like them. You may be close to the Mother, but to me you are completely rude and I pray not to be like you! So I will have to think about which house I want to learn from!"

"That was not a wise thing to say!" he fumed in return, "It will go straight to the Mother!"

"Fine," I thought, "If She is the Mother of All Things, She already knows, and She has already forgiven me."

Then, Alexandro, who had waited so patiently for Francois and I to complete our third round, tugged on my dress, and as sweetly as ever said, "Viéni. (Come.)" I had forgotten I was with the boy. I had forgotten I was in Italy. And I had definitely forgotten I was standing on the front porch of the Mother's home.

I honored Alexandro's plea, and I semi-deliriously walked down the street wondering where we were going. We ended up at the bus stop in time to greet his mother who was returning from a morning of grocery shopping in Prato. Alexandro frantically explained to her all that was happening, and now she was angry. "You will stay with us!" she said very firmly, "If you want to."

"Yes. I want to very much," I responded feeling tremendous relief as we walked back to the house.

Within moments of our return, a couple who was close to Amma came over to the house and a discussion ensued in the Italian dialect. In the end, dear Isabella looked at me with disappointment and said, "You are very welcome in our home, but if you want to see Amma, you cannot stay with us. I'm very sorry."

The wound in my heart deepened, and I did not speak. I felt lost in a storm of confusion.

A Desperate Plea

Eventually, I decided to leave the family's house that evening. I was not ready to give up the opportunity to be at darshan. I had given up so much just to get there, and I wanted to be sure.

I packed my backpack and arrived at the chapel with my belongings in tow. I was deeply sad. I do not believe I smiled the entire evening, and I trust it was obvious I had shed many tears that day.

When Francois greeted me at the door, he was as rude as usual. "So you decided to come?" he sneered.

"Clearly!" I responded as coldly as possible.

I entered the chapel and was given a seat in the very back where I could not even see the Mother as She gave darshan. I slumped in the pew and wondered what would ever become of my spiritual quest. I fidgeted the entire time debating why I had come. Eventually, out of a combination of boredom and desperation, I raised myself from my seat to kneel before the Mother.

As I walked to the center isle, my eyes fell upon Amma's light, and in that instant I knew She was real. Even with all of the doubt swarming in my head, my heart was electrified by Her presence. She radiated the pure light of God, and I could feel that Her presence blesses the entire world.

As I knelt down, I allowed Her hands to sweep my head onto

Her lap, and I was grateful for Her touch. When I was given the opportunity to gaze into Her eyes, I did not do so with the love and adoration of my first night. This time, I offered my frustration and despair. I knew She was an incarnation of the Divine Mother, and I wondered why She was moving me through a seemingly endless tunnel of darkness.

Accompanied by the fire of my soul and the passion of my quest, I looked into Her eyes and with my thoughts I demanded to know, "Are You with me or not? Are we in this together? I'm really doing my best, and I need Your help! I need to know if You are here for me!"

I felt absolutely desperate.

Afterward, I returned to my seat, only to find myself fidgeting throughout the rest of darshan. I felt jealous of those around me who sat so still in what seemed to be an ocean of peace and reverence.

Prison Lights

After darshan, two Swedish women I had met at Amma's walked me to my hotel in a nearby village. As I entered the front door of the small pension, I hated it instantly. The woman in charge was sticky sweet on the outside and outraged on the inside. I did not appreciate her fake words of welcome or her facade of love.

She led me to a small room in the basement. As I shut the door behind me, I dropped my backpack and immediately walked across the room to draw the curtains. I was horrified to find bars on a tiny, high window. It reminded me of a prison cell. I lay on the bed in despair and feared I would never be able to sleep in such a lonely place. Eventually, I lured myself to the dream state by closing my eyes and pretending to be in the neighbors' home. I was soothed by my imagination and the morning came quickly.

I awoke in the prison cell and realized my situation was ridiculous. I wanted to sleep on the earth. I packed my belongings and went upstairs to breakfast.

When the signora saw my packed bag, her sticky sweetness instantly melted. "Why are you packed? On the phone you said you would stay three nights!"

"I want to camp," I responded.

"You must stay here!" she declared.

"I will leave just after breakfast," I said firmly.

I appreciated her harshness because it matched her energy. It was the first hint of honesty I had felt from her. She yelled at me all throughout breakfast which I found vaguely charming.

The angel of the moment was her husband, a kind old man who seemed to be able to see through everything. Each time the signora left the room, he gently smiled at me or touched my hand, as if to say, "It is all in perfect order. This too is part of the Plan." I liked him immensely.

When I finished eating, I opened my purse to count all of my Italian Lira. I wanted to see how much currency I would have left after paying her for one night. I never did find out. As she saw me counting the money, she came and with a swoop of her hand gathered all of the paper lira I had, and said, "This will be fine!"

"But wait!" I protested, "That is definitely more than one night's stay!"

"The price was cheaper per night when you were staying three nights. This will be fine for one night's stay," she declared.

I was stunned. My world was getting more surreal every moment. I could not believe this was happening. Under usual circumstances, it would have been easy for me to stand up for myself, but in that moment, I did not have any fight left in me. I was too worn down.

I picked up my bag, offered a very sincere farewell to the beautiful man and walked out the front door with only a few coins. The woman had given me the general direction of the campground, but yelled after me, "It is too far to walk. You'll never get there!"

I did not care. I just wanted to be out of prison.

I found myself walking along a highway. I had never hitch-hiked before, and I was in a fairly desolate area. I was not sure what to do, and so I prayed. I walked and prayed and felt grateful to be outside.

I knew it was not a good time to think. My fear had a perfect opportunity to venture on a rampage, and I could not bear to go through that now. "Just walk, don't think," became my mantra.

Soon enough, a small car pulled over and a gentle, young man offered to give me a ride. He brought me to a combination hotel-campground that rested in a secluded area, tucked away from the villages.

The woman at the front desk was kind, and I was grateful to have found a home for the night. I unrolled my sleeping bag right near the stream, and I rested until darshan.

The walk to the chapel was exquisite. It was on a small, desolate path that curved against the side of the mountain and offered spectacular views of the countryside. The journey was a gift in itself.

Once in darshan, I still had doubt, rage and wounded pride flowing through me, yet I could not deny that I was in the presence of an incarnation of the Mother of All Things. Her brilliance was undeniable. Even though my frustration was mounting, in an odd way, so too was my faith.

I bowed before Her with a combination of reverence, disbelief and desperation. As I gazed into Her eyes, I begged for mercy.

After darshan, I walked back to the campground and crawled into my sleeping bag. I felt absolutely blessed to be cradled between the earth and the stars, the Mother and the Father. I slept soundly that night.

The Angels Descend

The next morning, around ten o'clock, I began to stir in my sleeping bag, and I opened my eyes to find a number of people peering at me. A few men and women had gathered around my campsite. I was most struck by one man who stood before his family facing me with his arms folded, as though he was ready to defend them if necessary. Possibly, to them I was an odd sight, but I was certainly not dangerous. I was a young, American woman lying on the ground amidst a sea of elaborate motor homes occupied predominantly by retired Italians. I could have easily soothed their fears with a simple, "Good morning," but instead I crawled out of my bag and sat on the edge of the stream with my back to them.

Two brave souls eventually approached me. A six-year-old Italian girl, named Melodia, and her little cousin became my friends. We asked each other a few questions, but in the end, Melodia was content to simply sing to me the only English words she knew. With a voice of an angel, she sang over and over again, "Good morning, good morning. I love you, I love you." Her song filled my heart with peace.

A couple of hours passed, and I realized I needed to go to a bank because I only had a few coins of Italian Lira and it was not enough to pay my camping bill.

I walked through the parking lot of the campground-hotel and a vibrant English woman with an effervescent personality approached me, asking, "Weren't you at Amma's last night?" She and I talked a bit. Her name was Barbara, and she was very friendly, but I did not feel like talking. I only wanted to rest. I noticed she had a car.

"Are you driving to town today? I'm looking for a ride to the bank."

"I'm not," she responded, "But I'm going in with my friends. I'll ask them if we can give you a ride."

We parted, and a little later she found me to say I could meet her and her friends in the parking lot at two o'clock for a ride to town.

I was relieved to have a ride to the bank, and angry I had to go at all. As I waited for my ride, I lay on my sleeping bag near the stream. A group of Amma's visitors who were staying at the hotel began to gather by the water. I pretended to be asleep as I heard them speak of the amazing miracles and gifts that had been showered upon them since they had connected with the Mother. They spoke about their lives improving dramatically and their prayers being answered.

As I listened to the personal experiences, I knew they were true and very much from the heart. Yet, there I was laying on the ground by the stream having been tossed out of the neighbors' house, yelled at by Francois, and stolen from by the inn keeper. I had very little food, because I had left most of my groceries with the neighbor family, and I did not have enough Lira to pay the equivalent of four dollars for my camping bill. Most significantly, my entire spiritual path had been invalidated by the simple words from Jyoti, "Mother says you should not follow the guidance you receive in meditation."

I knew the miracles around Amma were abundant, but they did not seem to be flowing my way. I was being devoured by darkness.

Soon enough two o'clock came, and in the parking lot I found Barbara with her two friends who were a couple in their fifties. Like Barbara, they were quintessentially British. Maybe it was my mood or my California casualness, but they struck me as being incredibly uptight.

The car ride to town was painful for me. The three of them spoke with a formality that only heightened my exasperation. I could not believe I was stuck in a car with three rigid British people simply because I did not have the equivalent of four dollars in Lira. "God, help me!" I thought as I wondered if I would ever find my way out of this seemingly endless nightmare.

As we rambled down the windy road, I remembered that in all of my previous travels, the only country I had ever had strikingly difficult experiences in was England. The British and I did not seem to get along. As I rode in the car I wondered if it was because they are so proper and I am so rebellious.

At one point Anne said to Barbara, "Yes, your life has been going through quite a transition lately." I knew instantly that Barbara's husband had left her, and in a vain attempt to soothe my agitation, I wanted to blurt out, "Did your husband leave you?" Possibly, I wanted to shock them, yet the thought did not leave my lips.

Instead, I did my best to chat politely about the job I had recently left and whatever other topics were asked about, but inside I was steaming. Finally we arrived at the bank and then ventured to the supermarket.

After I finished buying groceries, I found the three of them walking to the river. The couple had some old bread and Anne wanted to feed the ducks. I was charmed by Anne's love for the winged ones. She seemed entranced by their colors and movements. I wished I shared her joy, but in my pain, I was not interested in the ducks, the river, or the company. I wanted to return to the campground.

We walked back to the car, and I thought to myself, "Thank God. We're returning."

In the next instant, Anne's husband, Michael, noticed a cafe near the car that had tables out front. "Do you mind stopping for a bit of cappuccino?" he politely asked all of us. The two other women thought it would be "lovely" to stop for a drink, while I wanted desperately to get back.

The angst inside of me wanted to yell, "I am unwilling to sit for coffee, I am unwilling to talk and I am unwilling to be nice!" But I could not say it. These people had been kind enough to help me with my errands, and I simply could not get the words out of my mouth.

We sat down and I did not order anything. I would have, but I had very little money, and I did not want to spend what I had left on an unnecessary drink.

Once we settled in, Michael gently asked me, "How did you come to Amma?" His question was sweet and sincere, yet inside, I felt I was going to explode from frustration, and in a sense, I did.

Rather than offering my usual answer which was, "I felt drawn to come," the anger inside of me channeled itself into the truest answer. "She appeared to me in meditation and asked me to come," I said.

I felt an instant sense of relief as I spoke. It was as though I was no longer fighting so desperately to pretend to feel or be other than who I was. My desire to scream was satisfied by speaking those simple words.

The three of them were instantly curious about my response.

My eyes were focused on Michael since he had asked the question. He leaned forward with a sense of excitement, as though someone had set a gift before him.

"Will you speak more about that?" he asked.

Then, the concern that always arises for me when I speak the truth of my path presented itself, and I thought, "Possibly, I've said too much." I returned this man's gaze with the intention of quickly changing the subject, yet as I looked directly into his eyes, the most amazing sensation of safety flowed through my body. In that moment, I knew I was completely safe to share my path with him. I did not know if he would believe it or understand it, but I knew I could tell him the truth of my tale.

I looked at the two women who sat to my left, and the same feeling of openness filled my cells. I knew my greatest treasure, which was my connection to the world of spirit, was safe in their hands.

Within moments, I found myself talking with these three strangers as though they were dear friends. I shared without reservation and I talked for far too long about the stories of the Mother coming to me and the adventures of my path.

It was thrilling for me. I loved more than anything my connection to the etheric world, and it was also the part of myself I had learned to keep most deeply hidden. The torment of being criticized for an unbelievable gift had become too great, and I had learned to stay very quiet about that which I treasured most dearly.

My stories continued until we decided to drive back to the campground-hotel. In the car ride, I said a silent prayer that these people would become part of my spiritual family. I prayed they would become friends I could turn to in times of great joy as well as times of tremendous despair. Ones with whom I could share my journey, without fear of judgement or shame.

We separated at the parking lot, and I ventured to the campground as they walked into the hotel. We met again that evening when Amma's guests were gathering at the chapel door.

Convening for darshan can resemble a sporting competition. Most people are anxious to have seats near the Mother and some of us try to be subtle about pushing our way toward the door. As I chatted with other visitors at the front of the group, I noticed the British couple standing way in the back. They were waiting patiently without any need to try to jockey a good position.

"How amazing," I thought to myself as I wandered toward the back to say "hello."

When I reached them, Michael handed me his business card with their home address and telephone number handwritten on the back. They told me it would be a pleasure if I chose to visit them someday in England, and they welcomed me to call them if I ever needed help. I was very touched.

I thanked them sincerely, and after we chatted a bit I explained that I wanted to be in the front of the line so I would have a better chance at being seated near the Mother.

"Of course," Anne offered gently, "Go up toward the front."

As I was seated in darshan, I watched the couple enter the church. They walked in with an air of reverence, and they began wandering toward two seats in the back when Jyoti approached Anne. I watched Anne's surprise as she and Michael were offered what I call the two crown seats. There are two seats just to the side of Amma that seem to be reserved for special guests, and they offer a spectacular view of the Mother. The couple sat down and I could feel their sense of wonder and deep appreciation at the honor of being invited to sit there.

My seat, which was further in the back, faced theirs, and I had a perfect view of their profiles. I watched them on occasion throughout darshan, and it was interesting to observe them. I was entranced by their simplicity and humility. Other than Amma, they were the two most humble human beings I had ever witnessed. As my curiosity about them mounted, I glanced at the business card Michael had handed me. It was a gray card with silver lettering. It had four different phone numbers on the front, and three styles of Asian lettering on the back. By the looks of the card, he was associated with an impressive company, and his position read, "Chairman."

I had met many Chairmen and Chairwomen of large companies, some internationally recognized, when I had worked for a major charity my first three years out of college. I could not begin to associate this couple with the others I had met. She wore a long, simple sun-dress that looked to be home-sewn. He too was dressed in simple, modest clothes, and they both wore Birkenstocks. I remembered that when I had first met them in the parking lot and realized I would be taken to town by a middle aged British couple, I felt a small sense of hope when I noticed their shoes.

Yet it was not their clothing that made them so modest, it was the energy they radiated. It was their willingness to sit in complete reverence before the Mother of All Things.

When darshan was over, the couple offered me a ride back to the campground. I was happy to be in their company again and thrilled to be in the car. They drove an Alfa Romeo they had rented at the airport. I can still picture it perfectly. It was a beautiful black sedan with beige, leather seats, and it was striking because it was brand new. It had an air of perfection to it, and I felt grateful to be in such a comfortable car. I remember thinking that even if I became a slave to poverty, I could sit in a car like that one every so often, and I would be relieved from the horror of my situation, at least temporarily.

When we returned to the campground-hotel, they asked if I had a guidebook on Italy. It was a sweet question and it made me laugh inside. My life had been an absolute whirlwind before the trip to Amma's. I had been so consumed in releasing all that I felt kept me safe and equally consumed in keeping my fear at bay that I did not even bother with the usual details of travel.

When I told them I did not have one, they offered me theirs, saying they really did not need it because they would be returning to England the following morning. We walked into the hotel lobby and Michael went upstairs to their room to get the book. When he returned and handed it to me, it had a weight to it that was extraordinary. It was not a physical weight, but a spiritual one, as though I had been handed a holy book.

"There is something in this book for me," I said, "I can feel I will find something very meaningful inside."

"How strange to think that of a common travel book," I thought to myself, and then I said aloud in a joking manner, "Maybe I will find my answer in here."

Michael looked slightly embarrassed, as though he had been caught. "You will find something in there for you from both of us. It is a gift, and you must think nothing of it." He opened the back of the book to display a stack of Italian Lira, which was plenty to ensure I would travel comfortably through the rest of my journey.

"Oh my God!" I exclaimed.

"It is nothing. Really, it is nothing," Anne assured me.

The money looked like a shower of gold. Even more than the physical comfort it would bring for my trip, it was a symbol of the truth of the Mother's words, "I will take care of you. Trust Me." A sense of hope erupted within me. Maybe I was on the right path after all, and maybe I would find my way out of this seemingly endless ordeal.

I was absolutely grateful for the gift, and for the sense of faith it inspired. I thanked the strangers profusely before I left the lobby to find my campsite. The couple would leave extremely early the next morning, and as I lay by the stream, I prayed that someday I would see them again.

The Waters of Venice

The following morning, I awoke with the same sense of awe I had gone to sleep with. As amazement coursed through me, I packed all of my belongings. The first weekend of darshan with Amma was complete. I had seen Her four evenings and survived. While acknowledging the blessings of spirit, I still felt a sense of trepidation. I was not yet through the fog, and I knew it.

Before I had left for Italy, I had learned there was a palace near Venice I was to go to. I did not know the name of the palace, its architecture, or even its exact location, only that it existed and I would be guided to it. Through my meditations, I understood I had lived there in a previous lifetime, and I was to visit it now to clear some karma I had created back then. I did not ask for details of that lifetime, but I was quite sure I was not the saint of the grounds.

The last evening at darshan I met an Italian woman who lived just outside of Venice, and she had offered me a ride to the area. Her name was Claudia. She had reddish-brown hair and was small compared to my five foot eight inch frame. She was in her mid-thirties and newly divorced. She had recently spent a year living in Johannesburg, South Africa, which she described as "thrilling." She loved the excitement of living on the edge of life and death, and it was clear we would get along very well. She spoke beautiful English, and we easily shared with each other our deep secrets, dreams and fears. By the time we reached Venice, four hours later, she felt like an old friend.

Rather than dropping me off at the campsite, she brought me to her home, where I stayed for three days. During our time together, I told her the tale of being asked to leave the neighbors' house, encountering the wrath of Francois, spending the night in the hotel-prison, being robbed by the inn keeper and then being gifted by two strangers.

My new friend felt the Mother had led me through such a trial to help me release false pride. She suggested I held too much arrogance, and possibly the Mother was trying to humble me a bit. She referred to my arrogance as "princess" energy, and I watched Claudia in her exquisite beauty parade around her kitchen imitating me being a princess. "I have arrived," she said dramatically, "And the people have come to greet me."

I laughed at her imitation and even more so at myself. I also remembered the Mother's words the second time She appeared to me: "You must learn obedience first. Then humility."

Palace Karma

I hoped to forget about the mystery palace, but I made one fatal flaw: I mentioned my assignment to Claudia, and she absolutely insisted that I find it. She felt it was a critical step for me to release my princess energy.

With Claudia's encouragement, I entered into meditation one morning and asked to see the palace. I saw an image of a large rectangular structure with a bold clock tower and a prominent, arched doorway. I learned that a dark energy surrounded the palace. This darkness had descended upon the grounds during the time I had lived there, and my prayers at the site would help lift it.

Claudia gave me very explicit directions to the largest bookstore in Venice. She even handed me a boat pass and phone tokens. She wanted to be sure I did not have a single excuse not to find the location of the palace. While she worked, I ventured into town. Her directions were far too good to get lost, and after traversing the canals of Venice, I soon found myself in front of a beautiful bookstore.

Inside, a helpful sales woman brought me three illustrated books of palaces, villas and castles in the Venice region. I held all three books and knew the picture I was looking for was at the end of the largest book. In my rebellion, I looked through the other two first. Finally, I came to the end of the third book, and my eyes fell upon a two page, color photograph of the palace I had seen in my meditation. It was located on the western edge of the Venice region.

After a wonderful three day stay at Claudia's, I took the train west to the town that hosted the palace. I would pray at the palace before returning to another four evenings of darshan with Amma.

At the appropriate stop, I departed the train and followed the crowd of people to the downtown area. It was lunch time, and the streets were filled with locals on their afternoon break. The patio restaurants were packed and people were laughing and talking all around me. Hosts stood at the entrances to the restaurants and called to those passing by to join them for lunch. The town did not seem very dark at all.

After I bought some fruit and bread, I asked a shop keeper for directions to the palace. He complied yet seemed to think it was odd I would want to go there.

As I followed his instructions and came closer to the palace, the streets became desolate. The businesses were closed down and large red signs reading, "For Rent" hung in the windows. I did not hear talking or laughing, and I passed only a handful of people in the streets.

When my eyes fell upon the palace, I was struck by its tremendous size and by the air of darkness around it. I felt an excruciating pain in my heart and immediately began to pray for my own healing, the healing of others involved, and for the energy of the palace itself.

Suddenly, my body felt as though it had weights pulling it down. I desperately wanted to lie on the earth, and I walked around the palace to look for a peaceful spot. On the backside, I found a well-kept walking garden and I lay down under a tree. I had planned to eat my lunch in the shade, but I was no longer hungry.

A few moments after I settled onto the earth, my prayers intensified. Then, in an instant, an energy that felt like a bolt of lightning flashed through my cells. As it passed through me, it took with it the heaviness in my body and the ache I had known in my heart. A moment of Divine grace cleared what had probably been years of pain.

I felt a sense of freedom and relief. I turned to look upon the palace, and it too seemed lighter.

After I offered my gratitude to the Divine, I thought to leave the area and continue the train ride toward Amma's, but I knew it was important to go inside the structure. I walked to the front and found that most of the palace had been turned into city offices, but one section was open for visitors. It included rooms restored in the old tradition. A charming man led me on a tour of the rooms. He described them all in detail in Italian. I appreciated his company, even though I only understood a bit of his descriptions. Rather than trying to decipher Italian, I focused on my mantra, "I am *Your* servant Mother, in *Your* palace." With every step, these words emanated from my heart, and I prayed deeply for freedom from vanity, pride and arrogance.

As I walked through the rooms, a picture of a wedding regularly flashed before me. I saw myself in another lifetime being married to a man in a narrow chapel. Although the chapel was small, the ceremony was elaborate, and the clothing style indicated a relatively recent time period.

The vision was of me standing on the altar, wearing a full length wedding gown. As I repeated the mantra, a huge stream of white light poured from the heavens through my body and into the earth. I knew I was healing the pain I had created in that lifetime.

As I roamed through the rooms, I wondered about the image of the wedding but did not want to distract my thoughts with it. I wanted to stay focused on my prayer. As I repeated my mantra, dark energy released from my body. The more sincere the prayer, the deeper the release.

As we neared the end of the tour, I was astounded to come upon a small, narrow chapel. It was decrepit from years of neglect, but it hosted the same structure as the one in my vision. Suddenly, the vision in my mind's eye and the physical structure before me melded into one moment of brilliance. And I realized that all of life is but an answer to a prayer.

A Humble Return

I spent the rest of the afternoon traveling back to Amma's. Once in Florence, I took another train to Prato. Then a bus dropped me off in the saddle village only moments before the Mother's visitors would enter the chapel. I ran to the church where I found the group assembled and happily stood at the very back of the line.

I clearly remembered the grace of Anne and Michael's humility, the humor in Claudia's imitation of me and the lessons of the palace. Once inside, I sat in the back row out of view of Amma, with tremendous gratitude for the opportunity to be in Her physical presence.

Darshan had barely begun when Francois came to the back of the chapel and joyfully asked, "Is there someone here who can sit on a pillow for darshan?"

"I can!" I immediately offered as I remembered there were cushions on the floor resting at the feet of the Mother. Over the last few years, I had meditated for hours sitting on a small pillow. I could definitely do it.

Francois's smile instantly faded when he saw my face beneath the raised hand. He rolled his eyes, and it seemed to torture him to invite me up front, yet he did.

I spent the entire darshan basking in the glow of Amma.

For my remaining three nights, I stood at the very back of the line and was miraculously given a seat very near to the

Mother. I did not fight or struggle, I only let Her choose.

One night in darshan, I once again sat on a pillow up front. My eyes were so fixated on the Mother that they burned from lack of moisture. I was entranced by the grace pouring through Her, and I would not allow my eyes to close long enough to soothe the burning. I was not concerned with the pain, only with the brilliance of the Divine.

During the second weekend of darshan, I spent some time with a few of the people close to Amma. I had returned to the small village with the prayer that I would be invisible, but I imagine the commotion I helped to create the weekend before was hard to forget. Some of the people close to Her made very special efforts to make sure I was cared for. One man offered me a ride back to the campground every evening, and a lovely couple approached me every day to ask if there was anything I needed.

I learned from these three people many things about Amma. I came to understand that the Mother does not speak during darshan because it is only in silence that the greatest teachings can be offered. Her only focus is to awaken individuals to the highest light, and She is not interested in anything less than that.

I came to realize Her work on this planet will be fulfilled whether She is known or unknown, seen or unseen. She embodies God's will and nothing can or will deter Her purpose.

In Her endless compassion, She assists every person who sincerely calls for Her help, while She will not create an organization around Her other than what is needed to ensure weekly darshan.

I was told one of Her desires is to stay in the small village, and to do so, She has promised the neighbors She will ask Her visitors not to disturb them in any way. For this reason, She requests visitors do not stay in town. I learned it was indeed the Mother that asked me to leave Isabella's house the weekend before, it was not Jyoti or Francois's personal request.

Through the stories I heard, I realized Amma is a full embodiment of the Mother of All Things as well as a human being. In darshan, I saw Her as the Divine Mother, but She was not human to me. I did not imagine She had feelings or desires or even a sense of earthly pleasure.

I mentioned to the man who drove me to the campground that I looked into Her eyes one evening at darshan with rage pouring through me and I demanded to know if She was with me or not.

"Do you think She felt that?" I asked timidly.

"Oh definitely," he responded, "She feels everything."

On my second to last night at darshan, I left a note of appreciation for Amma, Jyoti, Francois, and the other three who had assisted my stay. I acknowledged the immense task of trying to smoothly handle visitors every week, and I expressed my gratitude for their work. I also apologized for my actions that made their efforts more difficult.

On my last night of darshan, I sat on the floor against the wall of the chapel. I was gazing at Amma, when the man seated in front of me touched my arm and pointed to Jyoti. To my complete surprise, one of the crown seats was available and she was offering it to me.

the flames in the storm

A Living Nightmare

I spent the following day on the train traveling to Vienna, Austria. When I had made arrangements to visit Amma, I realized my parents would be traveling in Europe at the same time. I made plans to meet up with them for a couple of weeks to travel through what used to be considered Eastern Europe. My older sister decided to join us and we all met in Vienna and soon found our way into Hungary, Czechoslovakia and Poland. We got along well, and I was grateful to the Mother that so much of our past tension seemed to have fallen away.

It was amazing to explore a part of the world that was once closed behind the Iron Curtain. In the countryside, it felt as though we had slipped back in time when we drove through farming villages that used animals to plow fields. The major cities seemed both more worldly than ours with their grand historic architecture and more simple with their lack of international influence. The locals who approached us were always very kind and I was grateful whenever one took the time to tell us of their world.

The last country on our tour was Poland, and there we stayed in the quaint city of Kraków. Every day, we walked through the town square marveling at the architecture and the beauty we found along the way. When we arrived, the college students were in the midst of celebration, and so the city was filled with young people dressed for a parade.

A few days later, we traveled the short distance to Auschwitz to visit the infamous Nazi concentration camp.

From that day on, my life would never be the same.

I knew for a week before we arrived at Auschwitz that it was part of our plan. Every day I thought about visiting the horrendous place, and I comforted myself by remembering the Nazi concentration camps were horrors of the past. They were a terrible scar on our world history, but that time was now over.

The morning came for us to visit the camp. My family, knowing of my sensitivity, asked one last time if I was sure I wanted to go. I told them I realized the Nazi camps were all closed and I would be fine. My prayer the entire morning was that I would be able to walk through the camp without being destroyed by what I would see.

I am crying as I write this. And I am remembering that I had no idea what awaited me.

At the camp, old barracks have been restored into a museum, and each barrack represents a different aspect of camp-life. To see it all is a long journey, and one I was determined to make. I walked through the first barrack feeling horrified, but also distant. Each picture, each article and each story is horrendous, but my mantra was, "It is all in the past. It is all in the past."

Then I walked into the second barrack, and my eyes fell upon a picture of a young Nazi soldier standing guard over a prisoner who was hanging by his feet. The soldier looked young and naive, and the old man hanging looked tired and worn. I let that picture into my heart, and suddenly my world shifted in an irrevocable way. In an instant, all of the past came into the present moment, and I realized I was that Nazi soldier.

I do not believe my individual soul was in that man, nor had I necessarily met him while in a body, and yet I was him. As I stared at the picture, I knew that every time I judged another human being as less than or greater than myself, I was acting from the same fear that led Hitler to direct a slaughter of millions. Suddenly, Hitler and the Nazis were not individuals from a past time, they were creations from the same fear that lived in me at that moment.

The illusory veil of separation became transparent, and I realized the infamous Hitler I had studied about in history was no longer a being who lived outside of me. He was and is a part of me, just as I was and am a part of him.

I stumbled through the rest of the barrack horrified at my discovery. When I emerged, I found my family waiting for me on the steps outside. I walked to my mother, put my head in her lap and cried for what seemed like forever. I could not think or talk or move. All I could do was cry.

As I wept, I became aware of a man standing nearby who was praying with my tears. His gentle focus never wavered, and while tears did not roll down his cheeks, he was crying with me.

When I gathered myself enough to look up, I turned to see the face of the presence that held a space for my sorrow. He looked at me knowingly, and he did not speak as he rolled up the sleeve of his shirt to reveal the tattooed numbers on his forearm. The shock of the camp, the pain of my realization and the sorrow of the man who stood with me was all too much. I buried my head again in my mom's lap, and I sobbed until another layer of darkness had been removed.

After some time, my parents and sister wandered into the third barrack, and I sat with the old man, his wife and a young translator. Through the translator, the man who so sweetly acknowledged and honored my tears, told me the story of his life in Auschwitz. He described his work, his pain and his frustration during his young years as a prisoner of the Nazis. As I listened, the camp came alive with the people, smells and terror of that life. After some time, his wife shared with me a piece of her story; she too had been a prisoner. The experience she relayed was so horrifying I have never been able to speak it, and I probably never will.

As they offered me a window into that time, I listened without saying a word, for there was nothing to say. When they departed, I acknowledged with my eyes the gift they had given me. I wanted so much to say, "I am sorry," but I could not manage to draw the words from my lips. I wanted to say, "I am sorry for everything...for the horror of that past time, for the horror of the present moment, and for the horror in the future that has yet to come." I also wanted to offer my awareness of the role I have played in all of it, for suddenly time and space had melded together.

I wandered, somewhat hypnotically, through the rest of the barracks. I made a point to look at every picture, every display, and every terror. As I observed it all, I only had one question, "Where is God?"

Where was the Divine in the midst of it all? Where was the light I knew ran through all space and all time, every creature and every moment? I looked and searched and cried, yet I could not see it. All I could find was myself in every picture. All I knew was Auschwitz as an outer display of my inner terror. It represented every place inside of me that was not open to the light of God, and it was excruciating.

After the journey through Auschwitz, I sat with my family in a restaurant. I ate the same greasy fries that were always offered by the server when I mentioned I was a vegetarian.

I told my mom, dad and sister I felt I was a part of Auschwitz, not so much in the past but in the present. I described my insight with passion, however, it did not fall onto open ears.

"I simply won't take responsibility for something I didn't do," my mother retorted.

"But we are all part of Auschwitz in every moment we judge ourselves or another human being. It is the same fear which causes us to judge and it creates the same horror. There is no difference," I offered.

When my words were received with blank stares, I continued, "There is absolutely no separation from the casual judgment I have of a crazy person I may see on the street, and the judgment that led Hitler to try to abolish all people who he believed were less than perfect. I have not physically killed a human being, in this lifetime, but I have shot down dreams with a glance, and prayers with words too harmful to repeat. I do not claim to be lower than any other soul who has walked this plane, but I certainly cannot claim to be any higher."

Yet my words were still not heard.

So instead, I turned to my journal.

I spent the evening writing to the Divine Mother. I told Her of my pain, my understanding and my devotion. I promised Her my life, and I told Her I would serve in whatever way was asked of me. I wrote that I was willing to set aside my own desires and goals to serve in the highest. I relayed all of my personal dreams and then I offered them up to Her, possibly never to be returned.

The following morning after a walk, I found my mother in my hotel room. My journal sat before her opened to the pages I had written the night before. There were tears in her eyes and I could see the devastation in her face. She had been deeply concerned about my life since I had left my professional work and mainstream lifestyle three years earlier. She did not understand my spiritual quest nor did she support it. To my family, a spiritual quest was nothing more than the pursuit of fantasy.

Her reading the journal led us to have the same conversation-argument we had been having every few months for the past three years. In her hysteria, my mother made the usual comments, "Why are you throwing your life away?! You have so much potential, and you just throw it all out! It is tormenting to sit by and watch you waste your life." This argument now had a new twist, which was, "Do you really think there is someone up there who is going to hear all of this? Do you really think there is an invisible something watching over you?"

Through the tears that flowed from both of our eyes and the devastation that ran through our hearts, we communicated our mutual desperation, but we never came to an agreement. In the end, I offered the only response I ever could, "Mom, maybe I'm wasting my life, but I'm doing my best to follow what feels true to me."

A couple of hours after our devastating argument, my family brought me to the train station and then continued on to the airport and back to America. I remained in Europe with a broken heart, a confused head and a spiritual travel book.

The Churches of Italy

I had planned to return to the States at the same time as my family, but a week before they left, I extended my trip. This extension was not due to guidance, but to fear. I was terrified to return to New Mexico. I had nothing there to return to. I would not have a job, a home or any money. Instead, I decided to venture back to Italy. I knew the country quite well, and I felt safe in its haven. I figured I could postpone, at least temporarily, the inevitable.

A few hours after my family left, I found myself engulfed in a cloud of despair. "Is my mom right?" I pondered over and over again, "Have I thrown my life away? Did I give up everything for nothing? Is the spiritual path one of illusion, while the material path is one of pleasure? Did I make all the wrong choices?"

Even after the train carried me back to Italy, these questions tormented me. I was living in the darkest void I had ever known, unable to access my own guidance or my conscious connection to the Divine. I could not see through the despair, and I did not trust myself enough to venture safely to the other side.

I spent my time in Italy crawling in and out of churches. I did not attend any services. All I wanted to do was pray, and since I did not have a home, the churches of Italy became my altars. I often curled up in a corner on the marble floor where others could not see me. I held myself and cried and prayed for hours. There was nothing else to do. I would know in time if the Divine would answer my prayers, but for now I would only know darkness.

I had one glimmer of hope during this period represented in the Italian travel book. I never once used the thousand page paperback for practical information, but I carried it throughout the rest of my journey as a symbol that possibly the guidance I had received from the Mother of All Things was indeed accurate. Maybe She was guiding me, even through this period that seemed to be an endless tunnel of despair.

I thought often of the beautiful couple that gave it to me and of their actions and prayers of support. Some days I held the book and cried. I knew they believed in me and they saw value in my choices and in the path I followed. I imagined they had helped me so generously because they had faith in my journey, and I prayed they were correct. I prayed I was indeed on a path leading to greater truth and love, although it seemed to be one leading further into darkness.

I often thought of writing to the couple to say "thank you" and I wanted to but could not. I felt too much pain, and I had nothing to share except that I felt engulfed in darkness. They had been excited about my journey and I did not want to disappoint them with the truth of my despair.

Nowhere To Return

After two weeks of crawling through Italy, I flew back to the east coast of the United States to visit my brother and younger sister. Again I was afraid to return to New Mexico. I had received the guidance two months earlier that I would be relieved of my trials on August first, and so I did everything I could to extend my trip that long. Somehow, I thought it would be easier to be on vacation and to be further from the reality of my situation until the energy shifted. Of course, the truth of one's life is impossible to ignore.

It was a very painful time for me. I was in the position of knowing I had given up my past lifestyle and was filled with doubt as to where I was headed. My brother and sister's lives seemed to mirror ones I had lived earlier, and they served as blatant reminders that I could not turn back.

Like my siblings, I had an undergraduate degree with double honors from one of the top Universities in the world. Yet as I walked through the buildings at the University where my sister studied for her Masters in Civil Engineering, I knew I could not return to the traditional academic world. While I recognized that the Institute was the perfect place for her to study, I only yearned to escape the cement walls.

My brother had received his Doctorate degree in Electrical Engineering and worked as a researcher in a laboratory. His apartment was pretty with wooden floors and freshly painted walls, and yet again, all I wanted to do was escape. One morning after he left for work, I lay in the guest bed staring at the square ceiling, praying for another way.

I had worked for three years directly out of college fund raising millions of dollars for a well known charity. I had sat in board meetings with internationally recognized business people and worked daily with those who held traditional positions of power. When I began that work, I was awed by the superficial glamour, yet that soon wore thin, and I realized my job consisted of juggling egos. I had no desire to return to that type of work or that way of life.

I did not know what my next step would be. I only knew once again that I could not turn back, and it was far too painful to stand still. So my only choice was to move forward.

I was grateful when the airplane carried me back to New Mexico. After months of creating and then avoiding my destiny, it felt good to return.

The Light of Friendship

Upon my return to New Mexico, I moved into the home of a woman who became one of the dearest friends I have ever known. We had met only six months before my journey to Europe.

A few weeks before I had met Lisa, I received the guidance that I was to wear a cross pendant near my heart. At first it seemed like an odd suggestion since I did not associate myself with formal Christianity. However, as the days passed, I began to long for a cross, and I did not have one.

One morning, I entered into mediation to ask my guides where I could buy the pendant. I was told very clearly that it would come to me and I did not need to search for it.

Then, at an evening party of drumming and dancing, I was introduced to Lisa and my eyes immediately fell on the piece of jewelry she wore near her heart. It was a Celtic cross made of silver filigree with a center piece of polished garnet. The design was exquisite, yet the energy that radiated from it was even more magnificent.

"It is beautiful!" I gasped.

She held her hand to the cross as she slightly bowed her head and softly whispered, "Yes. It is."

The cross was clearly a treasure to her.

An hour or two passed, and I found myself once again face to face with Lisa. Again, my eyes fell to the cross and I could feel my face flush with light.

Then, I stood in awe as I watched her hands gently remove the piece from her neck and place it around mine. The cross fell just in front of my heart, and I knew it was the one I had been waiting for.

"It's yours," she offered with a blessing and a hint of sorrow, "It's now for you."

And so our friendship began.

Lisa and I are very opposite energetically, while our paths are strikingly parallel. We both believe my soul's essence represents light in the traditional sense, while hers is a brilliant display of the harmony between the dark and the light. Not the darkness that is evil or bad, but the darkness that is brilliant, passionate and very pure.

We became instant friends, and she immediately began teaching me of the power and grace of pure darkness. I had always seen darkness as something to be avoided until I met her.

Through her words, actions and presence, I learned of the radiance of the dark side. She described darkness as the womb, and the feminine place of gestation where all light is born. It is the unknown, and therefore, to many of us it is scary, but to her it is the beginning point of all life.

Our friendship had been magical from the start, and upon returning from Europe, I was grateful to be offered a place to stay in the one bedroom adobe home she and her four-year-old daughter rented in the high mountains of New Mexico. The three of us lived together in friendship, love and chaos. We shared moments of tremendous joy, insight and healing, as well as moments of absolute longing, despair and fear.

The house did not have any inside doors, so in a sense, we all lived in one room. We learned from sharing a tight space that the greatest gift we could offer ourselves and each other was the gift of staying in our truth and honoring our energy in every moment. If I felt tired, I soon realized it was best to rest rather than to try to clean the house. If I felt drawn to cook, the entire house flowed more smoothly when I did so, even if tending to the pile of laundry seemed more important. We began to see that every time we acted from a sense of need or duty, it created chaos, and when each of us acted from the truth of the moment, all flowed smoothly and effortlessly.

Lisa and I felt it was perfect to share a small space in order to learn more about evolving together on a path which we had both often walked alone. There is a power that is undeniably created when two or more are gathered with the intention of serving spirit, and it was time to walk together.

The Father

Soon after I moved into Lisa's home, I had my first conscious connection with the Father of All Things. As I had been lying by the stream in the campground near Amma's, I had heard others talk of the Mother's suggestion to commune directly with the Father. I had known about the Father far longer than I had about the Mother. I would hear about Him when religious people spoke, but I never imagined He was a Being for me to call upon.

Yet, with Amma's suggestion, I began my prayers to Him. They were much like my original prayers to the Mother. They were both sincere and detached as though I was praying to a phantom.

"Father, I am praying to you. Please help me on my journey."

Then, one afternoon, I lay on the dirt walkway in front of Lisa's home. The hot summer sun beat down on the dry cracked earth, while I was held by the shade of a small cedar tree. I tuned into the etheric realm to see that Amma was holding my feet and Mother Mary was holding my head.

"Oh my God," I thought, "This is going to be big!"

I noticed a circle of etheric beings around me. It consisted of Lisa and three other close friends from New Mexico as well as some of the guides I had known from the etheric realm.

Suddenly an eruption of white lightning flashed over me,

and a brilliant white form remained where the lightning had been. The Being appeared somewhat like a cloud, yet every imaginable color radiated just beneath its surface. An amazing sensation of bliss and power poured through my body. I knew it was Him. My prayer had been answered.

I do not remember His first words to me, nor mine to Him. I do remember His passionate laughter. It was a laughter that could shake the universe with joy. It was so captivating it completely consumed me when I heard it ringing through the ethers.

In His conscious presence, I had no doubt that the universal essence is bliss, love and joy. Not a hint of fear or despair existed in His brilliance, and I was enraptured in ecstasy. At one point, amidst the pleasure of the experience, my logical mind decided it would be a good time to make some basic requests. After all, I was communing with the Father of All Things.

"Will you give me what I need, Father?" I asked.

"Of course I will, my child," He responded.

So my list began. I explained I needed money to buy some land in the mountains of New Mexico and to build a round, solar home. I needed my own home and it needed to be completely paid for so I could continue my spiritual work without concern for my material well being and without the constant disruption of moving. I was very serious in this well thought-out request, and I would have continued down my long list of needs, but His laughter prevented me from doing so. He did not laugh to mock me, He simply could not contain it. It was as though a comedian had offered Him the greatest joke of all times.

"So that is what you need?" He asked through His uproarious laughter.

"Yes, Father, it is," I said in all sincerity, but His laughter did not cease.

While my logical mind sank with the knowledge that He seemed to have little interest in fulfilling my version of needs, my heart soared. He emanated a white light so brilliant it paled every color I had ever known. His love was unquestioning and unwavering, and His laughter filled my cells with joy.

I arose from the meditation immersed in bliss and feeling astounded at the simplicity of connecting with Him. Without a doubt, being in the conscious presence of His energy was the most amazing experience I had ever known. It also felt completely natural.

The Council

A few days later, I connected with the Father for the second time. Again, I was awed by His unwavering love, and again I brought Him my concern for my material well being. I explained that I treasured my etheric connection, yet I needed help on the physical level. I had very little money, I shared a tiny home with my friends, and I felt more vulnerable than ever before.

In response to my plea, the Father told me that a council existed that would guide me and direct my physical life. He said they would help with whatever I needed.

I was deeply relieved to hear this, and I asked Him where I could find them. He showed me a doorway, and He said they were on the other side.

I arose from the meditation because I suspected my connection had blurred. Could I have understood Him correctly? I loved the idea of a group of people who would watch over me and help me in my life. I just wondered who they were and how I would ever find them in the physical. Were they very evolved beings secretly hiding in homes beneath the earth? Were they people who could manifest in the physical and then disappear again? Is that why they were on the other side of an etheric doorway? Or had I simply misunderstood?

I concluded I must have had a bad connection, and I would disregard the information I had received.

Moments later, the phone rang and Lisa was on the other end. She and her daughter had traveled to Colorado for the long weekend, and she called to tell me of an amazing lucid dream she just had. She wanted to talk to me because she was concerned she had possibly gone too far out.

She described a dream in which she was introduced to an etheric council that she was told would help guide her in her daily life. As she spoke, I was astounded to realize we had parallel experiences that day, even while hundreds of miles apart.

Lisa understood the beings of the council to be Ascended Masters or souls who have graduated from the earthly dimension. She had read about those who had attained full enlightenment as humans and now work tirelessly to assist the rest of us and the planet in our evolution. These beings exist in the etheric planes, yet they have the ability to manifest in various forms on the earth. I had never heard of such a concept.

After our conversation, I decided to return to meditation to meet this group. I walked outside and sat on a mound of dirt in the shade of the house. I closed my eyes, centered myself, and immediately saw before me the etheric doorway the Father had pointed to. Summoning my courage, I anchored my light so I could travel through the arched entrance.

Once on the other side, the light pouring forth was blinding, and my eyes needed to acclimate to the brilliance. When the space came more into focus, I noticed a number of beings who looked like people standing in a circle. They all seemed to know who I was and they welcomed me graciously. It appeared they had been waiting for me.

My eyes then centered on a dazzling, golden figure standing in front of me. I had never seen a man of gold before and I was entranced by His brilliance. Almost hypnotically, I began walking toward Him. He was smiling warmly, and He held out His hands to welcome me. As I offered my hands to His and looked into His eyes of gold, I realized I was standing before Jesus Christ.

The golden light flowing from His presence engulfed me and filled every cell of my being. My only awareness was of bliss and the feeling that my physical body would erupt with the intensity of the light. The Christ explained that the Masters were pleased to work with me on a conscious level and they would help guide my earthly journey.

Then He glanced to His right, toward the beautiful feminine being standing beside Him in the circle. I willed myself to the left so that I stood before her. Her welcome began in the same fashion as the Christ's. Her light began to overtake me, and this time, I was too overwhelmed to continue. I opened my physical eyes to relieve myself from the radiance of the meditation. I could handle no more.

My eyes refocused on the pine and cedar trees before me, and I felt comforted by the familiar setting of the physical world. Meanwhile, my mind was exploding in disbelief, my body was paralyzed from the light pouring through, and my heart was soaring.

I was enraptured in truth, yet I could not bear it. All I wanted was to lower the vibration of energy in me so that I would not erupt from the intensity.

I decided to carry myself to the car, and then I drove forty-five minutes to reach the first sizable town in the area. I blasted country music on the radio during the entire drive, and my only stop was in the largest, crudest grocery store I had ever seen. The neon lights, processed, artificial food and absolute zoo of commercialism helped to diminish the light that raged through me.

I wandered dizzily through the unfamiliar isles simply praying to regain control of by being. When I felt sufficiently drained of the light, I drove another forty-five minutes back to the house.

I was both disappointed and relieved that I had acted so quickly to drain some of the energy given to me that morning.

Darkness and Grace

The next day, Lisa and her daughter returned home, and I talked with my mom for the first time since I had been back in the United States. On the phone, I explained to her that I had made a decision not to discuss the details of my life with our family. I told her it had become too painful for me to meet with constant disapproval, and I needed a rest from the pressure I felt from them to alter my life.

The intensity of my mother's pain was evident. In my own desperation, I put a sword through her heart. I needed the little strength I had for myself, and I knew no other way.

In her tremendous pain, my mother offered the most gracious response any human being could have at that moment. Holding back tears, she said, "I understand why you are doing this. You have always hoped that we would learn to understand and accept you and your lifestyle, and we have failed miserably."

I was grateful for her response that validated my sorrow, and I hung up the phone feeling relieved that I had finally spoken my truth.

Lisa looked at me and said, "I've never seen you talk to your mom before. It's fascinating because I'm watching a hurt four year old. You want so much to please her, and yet you know you can't."

As she spoke I noticed my body. I was curled up on the desk chair with my right arm wrapped around my legs and the fingertips of my left hand clenched between my jaw. I was swaying gently to rock myself.

"My God," I murmured, "I am four years old."

"Something very traumatic must have happened to you when you were four, and a part of you never grew past that point," Lisa offered, with the wisdom of the shaman that she is. "How do you feel?" she asked.

"I feel there's something terribly wrong with me. I don't know what it is, but I know it's very, very bad," I cried.

Lisa invited me to rest in front of her altar, and with her gentle words and magic from above, she brought me back to a moment in my childhood that was so painful a part of me had died.

I was four years old, standing in front of my mother in our family home. I had a cloth doll clenched between my arms and the most intense look of horror ever seen on a young face. It was in that moment I was discovering that who I was as a soul was unacceptable to my mother's personality. My natural way was not appreciated, and if I was to meet with approval, I would need to pretend to be other than my true self.

The feelings of guilt, shame and despair that ran though my young body in that moment and my adult body during the healing were unbearable. I was ravaged by the vultures of fear, and the feeling that I was terribly bad engulfed my being. Every part of me cried: my physical eyes, the cells in my body, my heart and my throat.

I thrashed on the floor, and all I could do was scream, "I'm not all right! There's something wrong with me!" As the pain intensified, Lisa channeled every bit of grace she could to help me release the darkness in my heart that had become entrenched in one instant of absolute terror and a lifetime of turning away from my true nature.

The darkness within was a force created from the illusion of fear rather than the truth of love. It was energy that had become disconnected from its true nature of light. Its fire was fueled every moment I lost faith in the Divine, while it was smothered every time I honored truth.

At one point, Lisa knelt over my body and physically sucked dark energy out of my heart. She raised herself to spit out the energy she had collected and she coughed hysterically. I remember feeling grateful for her support and knowing that either the pain had to be released or I would physically die, for I no longer could live with it.

Then, just after the most intense wave of pain passed through, I felt a sense of space in my being, and I knew the darkness was leaving my body. It would only be a matter of moments before it would all pass through. In gratitude and exhaustion, I rolled over into a fetal position. Lisa gently stroked my hair and handed me a tissue for my tear drenched face. As she arose to pray outside, I heard her whisper, "Good work."

I remained curled up on the carpet. I was still a girl of four years old, and now I was angry. "Why are you so cruel?" I demanded of the dark energy that was leaving my body in waves.

"We are only doing God's work," the darkness responded.

I could not believe what I was hearing. "How dare you claim to be doing God's work!" I exploded in absolute fury. Then, in retaliation, I called on the light of the Father. His brilliance appeared before me, and I asked Him to reprimand the dark forces. His response surprised me.

"What they say is true, my child," the Father offered.

Then with a gentleness that was absolutely endearing, the dark energy explained, "God has asked that we respond to your call. If you call on darkness, it is our job to come. If you call on the light, the light will come. Every time you feed the pain of fear, fear grows, that is the law of this world. We are only following the law."

I was stunned. The darkness I had been afraid of my entire life was exposing itself as a simple servant of the Divine. Its essence is not cruel. It is our own calls to the darkness, our faith in it and our reverence for it that creates pain, not the darkness itself.

In a moment of gratitude and compassion, I called forth every bit of darkness I had ever known in this lifetime. The room instantly filled with dark beings.

I said to them, "You have done a very good job in my life. You have always responded to my call. I am grateful."

Suddenly, I found myself in the eye of a storm of celebration. The darkness danced and played and rejoiced in a moment of being recognized for its invaluable contribution to the whole.

"I am grateful to all of you, and I no longer want your lesson," I offered with gentleness.

The room cleared of all of the energy, and I remained as a four-year-old girl with the light of the Father. I curled up in His lap, where I sweetly fell to sleep.

A Promise

The next morning, I awoke feeling as fragile as ever. Since I had returned from Amma's, I felt like a babe who could not handle the reality of the physical world. I was twenty-seven years old, and I did not want to leave my friend's home. A stern glance from a stranger or a gentle question from a neighbor was often too much to bear. I preferred to stay in an enclosed area where I felt protected from all foreign elements.

Remembering the regression of the day before, I went to the Father in meditation. His radiance appeared before me, and I asked Him in all sincerity, "Is there something wrong with me?"

"Of course not, my child," He offered in absolute love.

"But Father, I do not have the courage to leave the house, or the ability to hold a casual conversation with an acquaintance. I believe there is something terribly wrong," I cried, "I used to be strong."

With gentleness, He explained that when He referred to me as a "child" I was to take Him literally. "When you visited Amma, you were birthed. This time, your birth was not a physical one to a genetic mother and father, but a spiritual one. You are now to be reared all over again, as a conscious child of the Divine Mother and Father, with the host of Ascended Masters as your teachers."

He explained I was to learn the lessons of the spiritual world. He promised that the Divine would guide me every step of the way, and I was simply to open to the teachings, as a child naturally would.

"You are an infant in this new birth, and that is why you feel so fragile. It is perfectly natural for a new born to want to feel protected by his or her parents. And this, my child, We offer you."

"Keep me safe in the physical world, Father. Please keep me safe," I begged.

"You are perfectly safe, my child, perfectly safe."

A Test of Faith

During the infancy, I spent most of my time at home or in the countryside immediately surrounding the house. I rested in the comfort of my friendship with Lisa and the brilliance of my meditations. I focused on communing with the Ascended Masters of the council. Through my connection with them, I received advice, healings, guidance and extraordinary love. It was absolutely magical.

I was deeply soothed by each communion with the Masters, yet I still held on tightly to one basic concern. The gift of Italian Lira the British couple had given me was gone, and I was only able to buy myself food because small, random checks kept arriving in the mail.

Every time I connected with the council I would beg them for help with my material life. The first time I did this, they said, "Everything is taken care of. You do not need to worry about your material well being. We are watching over every aspect of your life. Please concentrate fully on the work we are suggesting."

"What do you mean everything is taken care of?!" I retorted. "I have almost nothing, and that is not all right. I need money to live."

"Do you have food to eat in this moment?" they asked.

"Well, yes," I said.

"Do you have a place to sleep tonight?" they questioned.

"Yes, but..." I began, unable to finish my thought.

"Then you are taken care of. If either of these situations changes in any moment, please come to us with your material concerns. Otherwise, please do not use this connection to ask again about your physical well being. We assure you everything is taken care of," they offered with extreme clarity and amazing love.

Yet my fear still had moments of raging, and I asked again and again. Their answer was always the same, "We have said you do not need to worry. Please only come to us with material concerns if you need help in the moment, not in the projected future."

A touch of both humor and absurdity graced the situation when they suggested I enter a four month retreat period. The Masters were encouraging me to arrange my life to have as little contact as possible with the material world so I could concentrate on strengthening my connection to the etheric and learning the lessons of spirit.

The idea of a temporary retreat sounded sublime to me, yet it seemed impossible. I did not have enough money to last me four days, let alone four months.

As fear surged once again, I begged the council to guide me to material work. I had been led to all of my jobs the past few years by my guides, and I wanted the Masters' help now. I did not have the strength to search for work using the traditional means.

To my absolute astonishment, instead of leading me to a physical job, the Masters suggested Lisa and I take a road trip to visit specific areas of the southwestern United States. No other suggestions were offered, and I had nowhere else to go. As extravagant as it seemed, Lisa and I began arranging for the adventure. When I asked the council how I would pay for my share of the journey, they suggested I sell the three boxes of clothes I had in the trunk of my car.

One of the Mother's requests before I had left for Europe was that I clean my closet of all clothes I no longer used. When I argued with Her that I did not have time to do such a chore in the ensuing chaos before the trip, She explained to me that anything left unused and out of circulation creates stagnant energy. For me to welcome in the new, I was to clear away the old.

Days before I left for Europe, I tried on all of the designer suits I had worn religiously during my full-time professional career. The clothes represented an old way of life that was no longer mine, and it was time for me to release the symbols of the past. Many of the clothes went into boxes that I had planned to take to a used clothing store. Then, with my last minute need to move out of my home and the explosion of my car battery, I did not have time to bring the clothes to the store before my plane departed, and they remained in the trunk of my car while I was in Europe.

Now, with tears in my eyes, I drove my old car with its new battery two hours to Santa Fe, praying I could sell the clothes at a second-hand store and have enough money for a trip through the Southwest. As I drove to the city, I sobbed as I noticed all of the tourist stands on the highway that seemed to scream for a dollar. I felt like one of those stands.

I was humiliated by the fact that I was a well educated young woman who had fabulous work experience, and I was dependent on selling my suits to take a spiritual journey through the Southwest. I thought of my family with their well paying, professional jobs, and all I could feel for myself was absolute embarrassment at my life. The shame that arose was crippling.

I also felt terrified of releasing symbols of an old lifestyle, while having no idea how the new lifestyle would unfold. It was obvious to me I needed Divine intervention. I could not find my way out of this abyss all alone.

As I dried my tears, I walked into a second-hand clothing store to be greeted by an angel sweetly posing as a human being. Sarah was the new owner of the store and our connection was both instant and profound. I shared honestly about my situation, and she offered to try to sell all of the clothes I had brought in. She also gave me a one hundred dollar advance on the forthcoming commission.

Among many gifts, Sarah made me laugh. She asked if I would use my connection to the world of spirit to explore the past lives she and I had shared together. I told her I would definitely let her know if I was given any information. Then, I wanted to offer a beautiful and glamorous possibility and I sweetly said, "Maybe we were sisters together in the temples of Egypt."

With her flamboyant, Texas accent, she immediately and seriously responded, "Oh no, honey, I think we were whores together."

A Moment of Terror

As my journey progressed, light continued to flow into my life and the darkness of fear continued to flow out. When the illusion of fear arose to leave my body, it often felt very real. While I had released all that I believed kept me safe, I was still not totally convinced the world of spirit would take care of everything.

The day before Lisa and I left on our adventure, another wave of concern for my material well being flooded my cells. The terror was overwhelming, and in desperation, I lay on the floor to pray. Yet this time instead of feeling the familiar comfort of the Masters, Mother and Father, the messengers of fear attacked in full force.

I trembled against the cool, brick floor as explosions of doubt, confusion and despair erupted inside of me and in front of me. I heard the voices of myself and others, saying, "You are not safe to follow spirit, you must not walk that way!" Darkness zoomed in on me from afar, and a chill of horror coursed through my veins.

I was truly petrified, and I used all of my remaining strength to cry out loud to the Christ, "Help me, Brother, help me!"

Between the waves of explosions, I saw hints of His golden form before me. I knew His presence was steady, even though I could only see Him in fleeting intervals. He was sending me a stream of love and trying to tell me something, but I could not understand the message. I began sobbing hysterically, and His form and His message became clearer. He was asking me to move my body outside.

"I cannot move," I cried, "I don't have the strength."

"You *must* go outside," His voice commanded.

I began to think I might be able to move my physical body when I felt His form of light help me up. It was as though a gust of wind carried me to my feet, and I stumbled to the door as the Christ held me. I crawled onto the patch of earth just beyond the front step, lay down and cried. I felt a rush of instant relief as I nestled my body against the Mother's. Soon the fear passed, and only the grace of love remained.

A Tour of Grace

As the afternoon sun blazed over the open plains of the high desert, Lisa and I set out on our journey to explore parts of New Mexico, Colorado, Utah, and Arizona. We ventured down the road in Lisa's golden colored Honda, and I realized we only had a map, basic camping gear and about two hundred and fifty dollars. My head began to cloud with worry and doubt as I wondered how we could survive nine days of travel with so little. While we rambled down the dusty road, Lisa held the wheel, and I asked for help from the etheric world.

I closed my eyes to find the Divine Father before me. "Keep your bowl completely empty, so I may fill it completely," He suggested. Then, He offered a miraculous teaching.

In the etheric, I saw a simple bowl resting on my head. When the bowl was absolutely empty, the light of the Father could fill it completely. Yet, when I entertained a fear or a doubt, a lump of substance appeared in the bowl, and the Father's light could only fill the space that remained.

I watched the bowl for a long time. I noticed that if a thought arose, it did not become a clump in the bowl unless I chose to believe it. Absolutely any thought could run through my mind without filling the bowl if I did not give it power with my emotions, attention or ego.

When a clump settled into the bowl, I would say, "Please, Father, empty my bowl." Instantly, a ray of light would swoop down from the heavens and the bowl would be emptied. Then, I would feel centered in my heart, and the sensation of Divine bliss flowed through my being.

It was fascinating to see that everything happens in a moment. One moment, the bowl would be cluttered, and in the next it would be cleaned. It was all determined by the intention of the moment before.

"Please, Father, clean my bowl," became my mantra as we drove through the beauty of New Mexico and into the most magical tour I had ever known.

Lisa and I were committed to trying to keep our bowls empty and we invited the host of Ascended Beings to be our tour guides. On our first day, we drove into the night until we arrived at a small lake in the mountains. We stumbled through the darkness to find a flat space to unroll our sleeping bags. As we settled in for the night, we gazed up at the stars and reflected on the miracles of our lives. The moon traversed the sky, and soon our small area was lit by a silver hue. We realized we were camping in a circle of trees. The trees seemed to be as the Masters, surrounding us with their light and promising to watch over our journey. Their presence was a tremendous blessing and a symbol of all that was to come.

Throughout our journey, we turned to the world of pure light for guidance, and the Masters became our trusted companions and friends. We came to know those who accompanied our journey, and while each radiated a beauty that was astounding and a light that was breathtaking, they had distinct personalities. One was quite flamboyant and always appeared with a flare. Another was very simple and practical. Some wore clothing inlaid with jewels and others appeared in mono-colored robes. A few made us laugh hysterically. In all of their differences, it was obvious they shared a common bond. Their lives were dedicated fully to the light of God. Every moment, every thought, and every action was devoted to the highest good for all beings. They never swayed in their devotion, their work or their prayers, and they were always loving.

As we ventured through the desert, the Masters led us to perform ceremony, receive light and learn from the wisdom of Monument Valley, Chaco Canyon, Hopi-land, Grand Canyon, Canyon De Chelly, Pagosa Springs and some lesser known areas. Our focus was to welcome the truth of the Divine into our lives, and to invite the light of the heavens to fill our every cell, every thought, and every prayer.

The entire journey seemed to be otherworldly, as though we were living in dream time rather than in the physical dimension. Our lives became rituals in the ceremonies we performed and even in the lunches we prepared. We tried our best to move from guidance, and we were amazed to experience the ease with which our adventure unfolded. In the midst of the dry desert, all of our needs were met. We picnicked like royalty while overlooking amazing gorges, rock formations and rivers. We slept surrounded in the grace of nature and we laughed regularly.

For entertainment on the long drives, we sang. We told stories, prayed and wove visions of the future into our songs. Our lyrics offered praise to the Masters, devotion to God, and even a few thoughts to an ex-boyfriend of Lisa's.

I loved to sing and dance to the heavens, and during that period I decided I wanted to reincarnate as a Black preacher. I had once lived in a predominantly African-American neighborhood and my beautiful neighbors took me to their church. The sermon rang with fire and passion as a chorus of "Alleluia" echoed from the pews. I treasured the sense of abandon I felt among the congregation, and I wanted to learn to rage in that style of devotion. Lisa encouraged me follow my inspiration, and while she commanded the wheel, I offered the best sermon I could muster. I told the story of a child who continually asked, "Lord, are you with me?" as well as the Lord's eternal reply, "Yes, child, I am always with you."

As we received the gift of a rainbow after a ceremony, a vision after praying, and countless lessons in the stillness, I realized I could trust in the amazing journey of my life.

An Altar for Evolution

In the warmth of the afternoon sun's blinding light, Lisa and I returned to the familiar home in the high mountains of northern New Mexico. We were two different women than had departed nine days earlier.

I had five dollars and little food, yet I had no concern for my material well being, no shame and no judgment. The fear that seemed absolutely insatiable had passed through, and I realized the brilliance in the lesson I had lived.

I immediately entered into meditation and called on the Christ.

In all sincerity I said, "Thank you, my Brother. I understand why I needed to be with so little, and I am absolutely grateful so much fear arose in me because now it has passed through. I understand how perfectly the Divine has orchestrated this time. I am no longer afraid for my material well being. I feel thoroughly cleansed."

Then with absolute love, I added, "Now, I simply need some cash."

"There is work to do tonight. We will discuss 'business' tomorrow," the Christ offered in all gentleness.

That evening, Lisa and I unpacked all of the treasures we had collected from the trip. We arranged sacred rocks, sage and cedar clippings, Dineh (Navajo) beads, a rainbow Kachina doll and gatherings of white, gold, red and black sand to create an

111

exquisite altar to honor the evolution of all human beings.

The message after our trip was clear. We had virtually completed the death cycle of giving up the old world of a fear-based reality, and we were prepared to accept the grace of the new. Our focus was to welcome the truth of love into our lives so our seemingly separate worlds would meld into one. The Father would unite with the Mother, the darkness would come to the light, and the heavens would touch the earth.

A Gift from God

The following morning I arose early and wandered to the back porch to meditate. The sun was low, the air felt cool, and the stillness of the high desert radiated in my heart. I called on the Christ, and as His brilliance appeared before me, I gently asked about my financial situation.

"If someone offered you $10,000 today, would you accept it?" He asked.

"Yes!" my mind exclaimed in absolute joy, just a moment before my heart, surprisingly, cried, "No!"

I felt perplexed by my reaction. Then the Christ encouraged me to focus my awareness on the back of my heart. I followed His suggestion to find that area to be tight and restricted. I had learned the day before that, energetically, it is through the back of the heart that we receive. As I became aware of the density in that area, it became clear that it was not the Divine stopping the material flow, but me. Feeling dazed by my discovery, I walked away from the meditation.

An hour later, I returned to the inner stillness to learn more. This time, I connected with guides of light, rather than the Ascended Beings of the council. I asked why I was blocked, and they launched into a fascinating description of my experience as an infant and how that affected my ability to receive from others. They explained that as a child, many people approached me under the guise of love, yet due to their own unresolved pain, they really offered the dark energy of fear. These people were not consciously trying to hurt me, yet I was very affected by the darkness they emanated.

Instantly, my consciousness was carried into my body as an infant. I was lying in a baby basket as adults I did not recognize were leaning their heads toward me so their faces were close to mine. Although they wore smiles and offered sweet words, darkness oozed from them and onto me. They were trying to make me smile, but I would only scream. It was no wonder. Even as an infant, I could feel the contradiction in their being.

As I observed the scene, I realized that receiving had become difficult because I had learned it was painful to accept gifts from others.

The meditation continued, and after awhile I became restless with the length of the story and I simply wanted to be healed. I called on Jesus, and as usual, He was right with me. "You are getting distracted by the story," He said. "The bottom line is that you do not trust Me to receive from. You must be filled from the Divine, no other."

I asked him about a physical home on earth and food to eat. He asked if I trusted Him to provide for me. In that moment of consciously connecting with the Christ, I felt complete trust, and so I sincerely responded, "Yes."

Then He said, "When the gifts come, know the Divine has sent them. Gifts are channeled from God, and therefore God deserves the respect. All light is from God. Thank the being (who gave the gift) and praise the Divine. Do you understand?" He asked.

"Yes."

Then He offered, "The human element of fear creates manipulation and control around giving and receiving. Pure gifts are channeled from God. Anything other than purity is filtered through human fear. Your gifts will now come directly from the Divine."

I was awed by the extraordinary communion. I arose from the meditation and prepared breakfast in a daze of wonderment and faith. After I had eaten and the dishes were washed, I meandered down the dirt road to my mailbox at the entrance of our village. I could see Jesus smiling, and I knew my gift would be waiting. I opened the small metal box and on the very top of a large stack of mail rested a letter I knew held my material answer. I did not recognize the hand writing, but then my eyes wandered to the stamp which held a profile of a Queen. Before I opened the letter, I could feel the Divine had answered my prayer through the beautiful British couple I had met at Amma's.

In absolute amazement, I read the letters enclosed in which Anne and Michael each expressed their love for me, their faith in my path, and their willingness to help me in any way they could, including an offer to immediately wire me $10,000 from their trust fund.

Michael wrote, "Both of us feel Amma has sent you to us to help our own paths. I have not been able to tell you how stunned I was to hear about how you came to Mother - I was so amazed - it is the leap we all need to make." He also wrote, "We love and cherish you and please never feel afraid to write or ask us for help."

I had written one letter to the couple upon returning to New Mexico. I had told them of my torment after seeing Amma and of the amazing connection to the Father and the council I had experienced since my return. I also thanked them profusely for their support in Italy, and I wrote that if we never communicated again, I would always remember them as two angels who had graced my life.

Michael wrote, "Dear, dear Susan, you thanked us so many times in your letter it brings tears to my eyes. It seems the Divine is perfect! What we do to help you is absolutely reciprocated in what you do to help us.

"Ever since I opened your letter it has had a strange effect on me - my spiritual heart is more open and I feel more able to surrender. There is even a strange change in my body chemistry which I can taste."

The love and support offered in the letters was absolute proof to me that the Divine is real and all fear is simply illusion. Love reigns on this plane and we are graced by it's brilliance when we trust enough to follow its call.

I went into such a state of elation after reading the letters I could not sleep for thirty-six hours. I spent an entire night gazing up at the stars and thanking God.

I wrote back to the couple two days later. I told them of my recent meditations and the guidance I had received since I had last written. I gratefully accepted their offer for financial support, and added, "As Jesus asked, I offer you my heart-felt gratitude, and I offer God my deepest praise."

A Completion

Upon receiving the letters from Anne and Michael, I knew I had passed through a critical doorway in my own evolution. For three years I had been clearing the seven major energy centers in my body, one at a time, from the top, down. These centers are also known as chakras.

As I had been led to clear each one, my life had become absorbed with the issues of that particular energy center. When I had met Anne and Michael, I was purifying the first, or lowest, chakra which is at the base of the spine and symbolizes our connection to the material world and survival issues. When I received their letters, I knew I had completed a healing of that chakra, and I had concluded a three year purification process. I would certainly have more to clear in my chakras and in my life, but a major alignment had taken place.

I praised God that the process, which at times had seemed endless, was actually over. It was a major step for me, and while I had strayed many times from the light of God and I had stumbled profusely, I had passed through a tremendous threshold.

I felt extraordinarily blessed by all that had been given to me and all that was being offered. I prayed I would have the courage to surrender deeper into the grace of the Divine. I also laughed at myself because I knew there was nowhere else to go.

grace unveiled

The Retreat

As the leaves turned golden and the nights cooled, I arranged for my period of retreat. The Masters had suggested I dedicate a period to learning the lessons of spirit. I was to organize my life to have as little contact as possible with the material world and focus on my connection to the etheric. I knew it would be ideal to have my own place to live, and I turned to the Masters for guidance. I asked them to show me where to move, and as I quieted my mind, I saw before me an image of a round circle filled with light in the middle of our village. I knew from the picture that I was to live in a circular structure.

On an afternoon walk, I asked a neighbor if there was a round home in the area. He brought me to a yurt that rested nearby. A yurt is a Mongolian, nomadic dwelling that is a cross between a tent and a traditional house. It is made by tightening canvas over a round, wooden frame. This particular yurt hosted a raised wooden floor, all the modern conveniences, and was powered by the sun. My neighbor gave me the telephone number of the owner, and I contacted her at her main residence in southern Colorado. She agreed to rent me the space, and I moved in toward the end of September.

Once I was settled in my new home, I made all the arrangements to slip away from the outside world until Christmas. I wrote to my friends who lived both in and out of the area explaining I was on retreat, and I gave only a handful of people my telephone number.

The Masters suggested I be extraordinarily aware of the energy I invited into my space during this period. They asked that I interact with people who clearly and consciously supported my process. They advised me to take as few trips to town as possible, and they recommended I refrain from romantic and sexual involvement. The idea was to create a space devoid of outside influences and distractions so I could delve deeply inside myself and rediscover the truth of my soul.

The Masters also steered me toward consuming organic vegetables, fruits, nuts and grains since these foods were optimal for my particular body type. I stayed away from animal products, processed sugar, caffeine and alcohol during this period, and I never used recreational drugs. Another strong suggestion was to shelter myself from all forms of mass media.

The council was very serious about these requests. During September, before I moved into the round home, I stayed at the house of some friends while they were away. They had a home powered by solar energy that offered a television, a VCR and plenty of movies to choose from. My first night in the house, I decided to watch the movie *StarWars*. I had not seen a movie in months, and I felt it would be relaxing to become absorbed in another world for a short period. I remembered the Masters' suggestion to avoid mass media, but I watched the movie anyway.

The next morning, the solar power all throughout the house was dead. There was not a cloud in the sky, the sun was brilliant, and yet I had no electricity available inside. A neighbor came over to help me repair the system. After spending some time with the batteries and wires, he said, "I can't find the problem. I don't know why it's not working."

I knew exactly why.

After he left, I entered into meditation and offered an apology to the Mother, "I'm sorry I watched the movie," I began, "I know it was not in my highest interest. I *promise* I will not watch another film. Please turn the power back on so I can have access to the other conveniences this home has to offer."

Soon enough, the solar power was functioning perfectly.

Then, night fell, and I slipped again. As I had been looking through the available films the evening before, I realized my friends had the entire *StarWars* trilogy. That night, I felt desperate to see the sequel, and I spent the evening watching *The Empire Strikes Back*.

Unlike the first evening, I did not enjoy the film because I clearly remembered my prayers to the Mother. I sat with my mind observing the drama unfolding on the screen and my heart longing to follow that which I had promised. I went to bed feeling sad.

The next morning, the solar power was dead again. I was not surprised when it did not function for even a moment during the rest of my nine day stay, and it miraculously turned on when my friends returned to their home.

Another incident was with the radio. When I drove, I loved to listen to the country music stations. I had loathed country music when I had moved to New Mexico a year earlier, and I never imagined I would learn to enjoy it. Yet country stations offered the only clear reception on the forty five minute drive between our village and the nearest town, and so I occasionally tuned in. Soon enough, I came to love the gritty tunes, and my favorite part of driving became the country western songs. As the retreat neared, I had been asked not to use the radio, but I had a hard time resisting it.

Then one day, I put my favorite spiritual tape in my car's cassette player, and it stuck inside. Weeks passed, and absolutely no one was able to dislodge it. The tape played perfectly, the only problem was I could not eject it, and therefore I could not use the radio. For months, that tape was all I could listen to in the car. I understood the gift, and I was grateful to the Mother that at least She offered me the cassette I loved most dearly.

Good Company

Once the retreat began in full force, it felt as though I was living in heaven on earth. I was devoted solely to developing my spiritual connection and doing my best to follow the will of God. Most days, I meditated in the morning and received gifts from the Beings who appeared before me. Some days it was the Masters, and other days it was the Mother or Father who offered me love, teachings and guidance when I was still enough to receive in that way. During this period, the etheric world graced me with the most extraordinary healings, lessons and awarenesses I had ever known.

My company during the retreat included the few dear friends I openly communicated with, a handful of neighbors and the host of Ascended Beings. To look upon the Masters in meditation was an exquisite experience. Occasionally, they appeared to me in color or as a streak of light, but usually, they appeared in the form of a physical presence. As I gazed upon each of them, I saw all of the beauty inherent in a cascading waterfall, the tremendous strength embodied in the greatest of mountains, the wisdom etched in every canyon and the extraordinary light that radiates from all that is love. Sometimes, I closed my eyes and called upon them simply to bask in their energy.

Of all the Masters, it was the Christ I found most enchanting. I treasured the brilliance of His presence, the gentleness in His movements, and His smile that was so soft. I was enthralled with His energy and I could think about Him endlessly without ever tiring. I reminded myself a bit of a teenager in love.

The Christ was one of many Masters, and I wondered if I was most drawn to Him because of my family's religious heritage. As a child, my immediate family did not celebrate religion or spirituality, but my mother's blood was Italian with strong Catholic roots. Maybe, there was a remembrance in my cells of the Christian tradition. Possibly, that is why my connection to the Christ was so strong.

Crowning Glory

Very early in the retreat, I experienced a startling shift in my consciousness. As I meditated loyally, I acclimated more and more to the world of pure spirit. Then I seemed to cross an invisible barrier and the "unseen world" became more real to me than the "seen world." In the past, I had felt like a child of the material world with a doorway to the spiritual. Now, I felt like a child of the spiritual world with a doorway to the material. I also held the awareness that at some point, I would know the two worlds to be one and the same.

Just after the shift took place, I had a series of meditations with the Father of All Things. Each connection to Him was exquisite, and each offered me lessons, gifts and extraordinary light.

The first of the series occurred one morning after taking a long walk with Lisa. We returned to her home, and I practiced yoga on the back porch. After yoga, I sat to meditate, and I found myself in the etheric world kneeling in front of the Father. I was startled to see myself before His brilliance. I did not have a specific question, and I could not think of anything to say, so I simply bowed.

While my head was lowered, He placed the most brilliant crown I had ever seen on my head. The crown looked like the type a prince would wear in a classic fairy tale. It had peaks and valleys and was inlaid with beautiful jewels. The Father explained with energy more than words that it was a gift to help me attune to the purity of His light. It would remain on my head and assist me in aligning with the will of God. As we communed, I noticed my energy shifting. I felt simultaneously more grounded on the earth and more present in the heavens.

In gratitude, reverence and awe, I bowed again to the Father, and I arose from the meditation. Then I wandered into the house and I saw that Lisa was wearing the same etheric crown! I could feel it had been placed on her head in the same moment it had been placed on mine. She and I were so aligned in our work that when one received a gift, so too did the other.

That afternoon I was in town, and I could see etheric crowns floating above every person's head. I knew the spaces between each crown and each head were filled with fear, and I knew it will be a wonderful moment when all of the crowns come down to touch all of the people.

A Sliver of Brilliance

One morning as I reflected on my experiences with the Father, it dawned on me that in every meditation with Him, I appeared a bit older. In August I was an infant, in September I was a girl of four. In the crown meditation, I appeared to be somewhere in my teens. With curiosity, I entered into meditation to discover my latest age in the etheric realm.

As I settled into a still place, I found myself before the Father. Once again, I was struck by His brilliance, and suddenly my trivial intention for the meditation did not seem worthy of His presence. So I went into my heart and emerged with this request: "Please help me be of total service to You."

In the next instant, He pointed His finger at me, and my form completely dissolved! The body I had so identified with disappeared. I could feel myself before Him, and yet my form was no longer present. Then I saw that in the place of my body stood a ray of light. It was the same brilliant shade of white I had come to recognize as Him.

The Father welcomed me to come into His form. As a small ray of light, I began to travel all throughout the magnificence of His being. In doing so, I realized that I am the exact same light as He. I am simply a ray of His Divine essence. As I stood seemingly separate as a small light, and as I journeyed throughout His glorious being, I felt the exact same sensations of peace, bliss and joy. There was not a part of Him that was different than any part of me.

As I traveled in His grace, His words to me were very clear, "When you appear to Me, come as the light that you are, not as the human being that you think you are. When you travel in the world, travel as the light that you are, not as the human you pretend to be."

I agreed to do so. Then I asked to see an image of myself being connected to Him while walking in the human world. I explained I had moments of feeling frightened in my human experience.

"How can you be afraid when you know you are a piece of Me?" He responded gently. And I knew that was all I needed to remember.

Then I saw an image of myself in the world as a being of light with a cord always attached to Him. I remembered my pattern of forgetting my connection to Him, and I wondered if the cord was too thin. With that thought, the band grew to the length of my being, and I felt a huge rush of energy along my back. Then I was no longer a lone light with a connection to Him, I was a sliver of His brilliance.

Struggling to Remain Separate

As my meditations flourished, I sometimes questioned my ability to connect with the amazing world of spirit. It was hard for me to imagine why I had been honored with such grace.

One afternoon I saw a devout Buddhist friend of mine, and I asked her sincerely if she thought that Divine beings would appear to a young woman like me. I had only begun to open to the concept of the Divine four years earlier. I had no formal spiritual training, and I had enough fire fueling my temper to warm a small village.

She offered the most comforting response. She said, "It makes perfect sense to me because you're a great audience. You listen carefully, you respond sincerely, and you express gratitude. If I were them, I'd come to you as well."

Feeling inspired, the next morning I entered into meditation once again and I found myself as a small flame of light in front of the radiant Father. I was the same shade of white as He, and a cord of light connected the two of us.

His first words to me were, "So you *still* see yourself as being separate from Me?"

"Yes," I responded honestly, and He invited me to merge into His brilliance. I immediately entered fully into His essence, and instead of feeling the familiar peace I expected, I was surprised to feel discordant and rebellious. While I was consumed by His light, I found myself struggling to escape to be a separate flame. I tried desperately to push myself out of His presence, while He encouraged me to remain absorbed in His light.

I did not understand why I was so determined to escape, and then the answer was given to me. My individualized ego self was struggling to remain separate. A part of me did not want to completely merge with another, even the God of Gods. I was fighting to be different and to be my own, small self.

Inside I began to feel very confused. I knew in my heart I wanted to remember my oneness to the Divine, yet I was watching myself completely resist it. I saw myself wanting to be a piece of God, but wanting to be a separate piece. I was afraid of losing my small self in the vastness of the oneness.

I asked the Father for help, and He explained I was resistant to giving up my limited self for the experience of the truth of light. He said, "You believe you are giving up something for nothing, but in truth you are giving up nothing for everything."

I knew He was right, but I could not feel that truth in my veins. I felt frustrated and I decided to leave the meditation.

Peaceful Ecstasy

Two mornings later my resistance had not subsided; I felt irritable and restless. As I sat down to meditate, I remembered a promise I had made to a friend awhile back. I wondered how I could keep a promise from the past when the future was constantly evolving and changing.

As I closed my eyes, Jesus stood before me. In response to my quandary, He said, "It is not for you to make promises for the future. It is for you to be present in each moment and follow the guidance given."

While understanding His lesson, I found myself agitated by the strict tone in His voice and my inner turmoil transformed into anger. "Yes Sir!" I blurted out with the energy a disgruntled slave would reserve for a cruel master.

He responded compassionately, "I do not speak as though I am above you, I speak to you as an equal."

I began to realize how rude I had been and I immediately said, "Thank you, Brother," although my heart was not completely in my response.

Jesus, of course, knew that and He said clearly, "Do not thank me with your words. Thank me with your devotion to the light." I understood completely.

I settled into a deep and humble meditation. I asked to be with the Father because I wanted to try again to feel myself within His vastness, rather than seemingly separate. He was instantaneously before me and I appeared as a small flame of light. I immediately merged into His brilliant form, and I felt the familiar bliss, freedom and peaceful ecstasy I had come to associate with the Divine. It was a relief to leave resistance behind.

As I rested in His radiance, I realized that when I was absorbed by His grace, I was the entire universe. I was all time, all space and all light! When I chose to consciously leave His presence to be a flame outside Him, I was simply Susan and all of my past and limited incarnations. The few times I consciously moved myself to be outside of Him, I immediately wanted to merge back in. I no longer feared losing my individual self in the joy of His vastness. Suddenly, I could feel in the depths of my being that it is only when we know we are one with God that we are free to become completely individual.

Lessons with Laughter

As the retreat unfolded, my life was very happy. The simple pleasures of meditating, exercising, visiting with dear friends, eating and sleeping filled my world. I laughed often, especially when the lessons from spirit wove into my daily life.

A simple lesson was to remember to offer gratitude to the Divine for all that was offered in each moment. Before the retreat began, I had been tremendously concerned about my material well being, and I sincerely thanked God every time a meal came before me and every night I had a warm place to sleep. Until I had experienced such extreme financial limitation, I did not understand why people offered gratitude to spirit for something that obviously came from the supermarket or for a bed that was always available.

After the monetary gift arrived, I continued to express gratitude for every meal I received and for every night in a safe home. I had come to understand that absolutely everything is a gift from spirit regardless of appearances.

I loved offering my praise to God. There were times when Lisa, her daughter and I sat down to share a meal, and Lisa and I became so consumed in expressing our gratitude to the Divine we forgot that a meal was placed before us. Occasionally, before dinner, the little girl would say, "Susan, you can eat with us, only if you do not pray!"

Of course, there were plenty of moments when I forgot to

acknowledge the grace that surrounded me. If I did not pray before a meal or offer gratitude for a gift, the Masters sometimes appeared before me and gently teased, "You seem to be getting soft. Maybe you are a little too comfortable and a little too forgetful." I always laughed with them, acknowledged my hastiness and offered my praise.

A bad habit I had developed over the years was using the Divine's name when I really felt like swearing. Sometimes in a moment of frustration, I would hear myself yelling, "Oh God!" or "Jesus!" when I had no intention of calling forth the world of spirit.

During the retreat when I used Jesus's name in such a fashion, He simply appeared before me in an array of brilliance. I was always startled to see Him since I was not in a moment of revering the Divine, yet there He was with a slight smile on His face. "Yes?" He would ask, knowing I had simply slipped. While He reveled in His humor, I always blushed with embarrassment and immediately acknowledged the lesson.

Another laugh I shared with the Masters revolved around what I called my "remedial karma." Possibly because I needed my lessons to be extraordinarily clear, the consequences of my actions seemed to be instantaneous and blatant. If I judged another for being forgetful, in the next instant I would not be able to remember my own phone number. Or if I arrogantly described someone as clumsy, I would trip over my feet on the next step.

The Masters consistently asked me not to play in the world of false judgment since it immediately drew me into the illusion of separation. I imagine the Divine was attempting to lure me away from the notion of duality by placing me in the shoes of another immediately after I had held judgment.

One time I tried to trick the universe. Since I always found myself in a situation I had just judged, I decided I would criticize things I wanted. I stormed around the house claiming, "I cannot stand people who are fabulously wealthy or those of exquisite beauty. And people who find peace and happiness in every instant make me livid!"

My trick did not work, but it was a funny moment, and we all laughed.

A Hand for a Prayer

During the retreat, my sensitivity dramatically heightened. As I learned to acclimate more fully to the dimensions beyond the physical, I had moments of difficulty functioning on the earthly plane. I was fortunate to have very few material responsibilities since I was not always adept at handling the basic ones.

One day, the entire physical world seemed to be a blur, and it was difficult for me to distinguish details in form. It was not the ideal state for grocery shopping, and as I found myself standing in front of the bulk food section at the health food store, I wanted to cry. It had taken a tremendous amount of concentration to find the bin of short grain, organic, brown rice, and I felt overwhelmed by the next step, which was to put some rice into a small bag and label it with the appropriate bin number.

To prevent my tears and what I assumed would be the embarrassment of explaining to another shopper that I could not bag my own rice, I prayed fervently. I stood silently asking for help in front of the wall of bulk foods until I felt a hand clasp mine.

It had happened to me before in a crowded setting that a child had accidentally taken my hand, assuming it was his mother's. Yet, this hand was a woman's. I wondered if she had mistaken me for someone else. Then, I looked over to find an etheric Master standing beside me. She was so real I could feel the warmth of her hand in mine.

Her presence deeply soothed me, and I was slowly but surely able to fill a bag of rice and label it accurately.

Divine Flames

While I lived in retreat, my physical health, for the most part, was very good. I often felt strong and energetic. Then one day in meditation, one of the Masters appeared to me and said, "You are in fine health. You do not need to be concerned about your physical well being." The message seemed odd and unnecessary because I was not worried at all.

The next day, however, I awoke to a fire of transformation engulfing my cells. The etheric flames sent pain into every part of my body, and it was excruciating to move. I suddenly understood the message of the previous day. As the heat only increased in intensity, I found if I stayed very still, and in prayer, the pain was easy to bear.

The next morning, my body was still hot, but I could move around the house. I called upon the Masters, and they explained that as my soul evolved, so too did every aspect of my being. The fire was an abundance of light being channeled into my cells, and my body needed to use all of its resources to absorb and anchor the incoming energy.

From that time on, whenever a Master appeared to tell me my health was perfectly fine, I knew what was coming next.

A Duel

As I came to know the world of pure spirit as a haven of bliss, I still encountered discord in the physical dimension. While the Divine always showered me with love, my fear continued to create pain in my human experience. During the retreat, I turned to the Divine for assistance when I found conflict in my life.

One week, I happened to hear from a few different sources that a previous spiritual teacher of mine had told people that my path only brushed the surface. I felt incredibly hurt by the news especially since she had once been a close friend. As the reports of slandering remarks continued to pour in, I felt furious.

I entered into meditation and called on the Christ. In my anger I demanded that He do something about the situation. He did, but it was not what I expected.

First, He said He would not offer any consolation or advice until I very sincerely thanked the other woman's soul. I was livid at His suggestion. She was saying cruel things about me, and I wanted Him to scold her. When He refused, my temper flared and I stormed away from the meditation saying, "You are absolutely no help at all!"

However, my rage was unbearable, and I soon returned to the etheric world. Once again, I was asked to thank the woman's soul, and again in my fury, I refused.

That night, I tossed and turned, and I could not sleep

because of my anger. I finally realized my only hope for peace was to follow the Christ's suggestion. I swallowed my shallow pride, turned to the world of pure spirit and sincerely said, "I thank her soul."

Immediately, I saw a picture in the etheric realm of the other woman and me in a ferocious sword fight. We were certainly feuding!

As I observed the duel, the Christ said to me, "Do not fight!"

"She will kill me if I do not defend myself," I thought and continued to wield my sword.

Then I heard His words once again, this time with more force, "Do *not* fight!"

I knew He was right.

In the etheric world, I called forth my own light, put down my sword and sat in prayer. The other woman continued to fight madly, but suddenly her sword could not touch me. It was as though she had been removed to a movie screen. The screen was right near me and her actions seemed scary, but she was only an image and she could not harm me.

As I sat observing the scene, the Christ explained that the woman's words and actions, in themselves, could not hurt me. If I stayed in a state of love, I would receive love. If I fought back in anger, the poison of that anger would return to me. The universe always responds to an individual in accordance to his or her own intention, not to the intentions others direct toward them. As He offered me the lesson, I realized I never needed to fear another.

Then the Christ led me to a place of compassion. He asked me to see the other woman and myself as little girls. In my mind's eye, I saw the two of us as five year olds.

"You're mean!" I said to the other little girl.

"You're meaner!" she responded as a typical child would do. Then she continued, "You used to be my best friend, now you don't even care about me."

As I listened, I was stunned. I realized I probably had been her best friend. As a woman, she was very powerful and also quite guarded from others. I had probably been allowed behind the armor much more than most.

"I do so," I responded in sincerity.

"Nuh uh," she mumbled, "You just left me behind."

And in that moment, I understood the pain. I had evolved on my own path, and I no longer turned to her for counsel. As I saw the hurt in her young face, I knew it was only her fear of not being loved that caused her to act with such cruelty as an adult. Suddenly, it was impossible for me not to forgive her.

As we found harmony once again, the Christ explained that the fear of not being loved is the only reason one person ever causes harm to another.

That night as I lay in bed, I held a picture of my former teacher in my mind's eye. I prayed deeply and compassionately for the healing of her pain. Suddenly, I realized I was channeling my energy into a prayer for someone who appeared to be trying to hurt me. And in that instant, for the first time in my life, I felt true humility.

In gratitude, I turned my gaze toward the Christ as He stood engulfed in God's glory. An ocean of love rushed through me as I looked at Him, and I said, "You are my inspiration. You are my meaning. You are my reason for being."

While I drifted off to sleep, He sweetly responded, "As you are Mine."

A Dance

One of the funniest Masters who accompanied my journey was a renowned and loved teacher of Tibetan Buddhism. I knew very little about this living Master before He appeared in my meditations, yet I was quickly awed by His absolute simplicity and equal brilliance. He proved to be the perfect mediator between me and my immediate neighbor.

I shared the private road to my home with a woman in her mid-forties who lived in a small adobe next door. Margaret and I had very little contact, yet when we did it was often with conflict. We regularly repeated a particular dance, and only the details varied.

One day after a ferocious rain storm had passed through the village, our dirt road resembled a swamp. Then a propane truck drove in to fill our tanks, and the large wheels left gaping holes in the earth. When the soil hardened, it was clear we needed help.

I saw Margaret one morning and she said, "I think we should call a construction company and ask them to level the drive. What do you think?"

I honestly responded, "I think it would be better to talk to the neighbors who have been here for a long time because they will probably know the best way to handle it."

"Fine!" she stormed angrily, "We'll do it your way!"

In a flash of equal fury, I fumed, "I don't want to do it my way! I want us to be able to express our opinions and then decide together what will be best!"

"Forget it!" she yelled as she began to walk off, "We cannot work it out. We'll just do it your way."

Every time we tried to settle an issue, nothing would get done because we could never come to a harmonious agreement. It was a ridiculous and boring dance.

The following evening as I bounced down the hole-filled road in my car, I decided it was time to meditate on the situation. I called on the glorious Tibetan Master, and He showed me all that occurred in our dance. I saw an image of Margaret handing me a package that symbolically represented her power. However, rather than accepting the gift, I let it fall to the ground and acted as though I would die instantly if it ever touched me. One would assume by my response that the package was filled with a horrific substance.

It was an awful picture of Margaret standing completely powerless after having given the package away, and me obsessing that the gift not touch my body in any way. I asked the Tibetan Master what I should do. He suggested, "When she hands you her power, do not let it drop to the ground and act as though it is the plague. Take the package and hold it in your hands as one would hold a great treasure. Marvel at it and say, 'Beautiful! Beautiful!' Then, hand it back to her."

I remember thinking it was silly advice and I asked, "What if she doesn't take it back?!"

He simply repeated the same suggestion.

I did not immediately act on His guidance because I only came to appreciate its value a couple of weeks later. One afternoon, I was racing through the house, and I accidentally jarred my right ankle. I had sprained it months earlier, and it still had not healed completely. I felt frustrated as I watched it begin to swell once again.

Later that night as lay in bed, I could see Jesus before me. My temper was as swollen as my ankle, and I decided to hand the Christ my pain. I energetically removed the sprain from my body, handed it to Jesus and said, "Here, it is Yours!"

To my surprise, Jesus held the energy as though it was the greatest treasure on earth. He looked at it in awe and exclaimed, "Beautiful! Beautiful!"

When I realized He held a treasure, I said, "Hey! Give that back to me!"

"Oh no!" He said instantly, "You gave it to Me."

Then, I yelled, "But that was mine!"

The moment that thought slipped out, I could see His knowing smile and I remembered the lesson from the Tibetan Master. We both laughed, and Jesus handed me back the treasure. I put it immediately in my heart, and I was grateful for the gift.

As I dosed off to sleep, I remembered I had once heard that the best way to heal a wound is to hold it in one's heart.

Chasing Illusion

The spiritual path is an amazing adventure. Amidst the blatant miracles I experienced, the plethora of doubt that had been stored in my cells continued to arise to be healed.

One day, I spent an entire afternoon feeling incredibly agitated and frustrated. Fear was raging and I began to question life and the meaning behind it all. Suddenly, it was as though all of the past meditations had never happened, and I stood in absolute perplexity as for the reason of existence.

I decided to commune with the Divine. The world of spirit would certainly carry me out of this lull and remind me of the importance of each life on this earth plane.

I entered into meditation, and I saw before me the Mother and Father. "Why am I here?" I asked with a touch of arrogance in my tone. I expected a flattering answer about the vital role each person plays in the whole.

The Mother simply responded, "As a child explores, so too do you. As a child gets lost, so too do you."

I became even more agitated by her response and I demanded to know, "Am I lost?"

She offered, "You are found when you remember the Divine. You are lost when you forget." I pondered Her statement, and then She continued, "The thrill of being lost is being found again. Soon the thrill of being found again will be relinquished for the eternal joy of living in full communion with God."

As I absorbed the truth of Her words, the Father added, "An aspect of the human condition is created to thrive on lost and found, rich and poor, good and bad. To this aspect of the self, peace, contentment, wholeness, and oneness are death, but in truth they are life. Trust this one point, and you will meld into the eternal bliss that you are."

Then an image of a typical chase scene from a Hollywood action movie flashed before me. I knew the analogy was that we become enthralled in the chase, while it is really the happy ending that we want.

After that thought passed through my mind, I heard the Father say with absolute gentleness, "Stop the chase. Stop the chase."

Devotional Heights

In this amazing period, the grace of my meditations flowed into my material existence. My prayers were regularly answered, and my physical world was full of miracles.

One day in the midst of such abundance, an unsettling knowing began to emerge from my soul. I realized that even if God fulfilled every worldly desire of mine, it would not satiate my being. Every wish and whim could be granted in every instant, yet that alone would not be enough. Even if I could consciously arrange all the details of my life to satisfy my momentary desires, I would not necessarily feel content.

Frustration fell upon me as I realized this truth. It did not matter how many more miracles I would experience, because in themselves, they would never fill me. I felt terribly ungrateful as these thoughts coursed through my mind, and I also felt disappointed.

I turned to the Father in meditation, and with discontent I said, "You could answer every prayer of mine in every instant, and it would still not be enough." I felt sorry my attitude was so ungrateful, but in that moment, it was my truth, and I knew there was no reason to lie. The world of spirit would immediately unmask any veil I tried to raise.

He surprised me with His reply. "You are absolutely right," He said with love. Then with a motion of His form, He said, "Come, let me show you."

flames *of* grace

In an instant, we traveled to a crystal city. I do not know where or when it existed, but it was magnificent. It was pristine in its beauty with perfectly manicured buildings of crystal light and enlightened individuals moving throughout. I was speechless as I looked at an example of perfection in form.

The Father explained, "In this city, every thought is for God. Every moment, every action, every intention and every instant is to celebrate the Divine." As He spoke, I could read the individuals' minds and I realized the truth of His words. I saw a woman setting a simple object on the wall of a turret while she offered complete reverence to the world of spirit. "It is the purity of devotion that allows the city to progress to such amazing heights," the Father continued, "The exquisite physical result will never fill the soul, but *the devotion to the Divine always will.*"

A Rite of Passage

During the retreat, there was a short period when I did not formally connect with the Masters, the Mother or the Father. My body ached, and I simply could not seem to bring myself to do much of anything. I decided I was lazy. With cruelty, I told myself over and over again that it was unbelievable the universe was supporting me to do spiritual work, and I could not even bother to meditate.

Fortunately, I eventually realized what was happening. I was simply too afraid to tune in. I had come once again to another illusory ceiling of fear and there was work I needed to do to pass through.

The state was familiar to me. Fear had arisen, and I had become too petrified to move my body because I knew movement would encourage the fear to surface. I was terrified that the darkness would be so horrendous it would kill me if I allowed it to emerge. So I stayed very still and eventually became depressed.

I was grateful when Lisa offered to give me a massage with the prayer that it would help clear away the layer of fear. She practices a unique style of body work rooted in an ancient Polynesian tradition.

As we began the session, the fear surfaced with great force, and my body throbbed with pain. At the same time, her touch completely nurtured, and so I simultaneously felt bliss and agony. About half way through the two hour massage, most of the fear had arisen and passed through, and I was once again able to consciously connect with the Divine Mother and Father. I cried in gratitude.

When the session was complete, Lisa explained that she felt I was being led through a rite of passage and welcomed into the mother phase of life. She told me that women have three phases in life: the maiden, the mother and the wise woman. While women live in all three stages simultaneously, there are certain periods in life when one aspect tends to be more prominent. She understood it to be between the ages of 28 and 30 that women usually leave the maiden stage and pass into the mother phase. I would be 28 years old the following month.

By the Light of the Moon

The next morning, I awoke early enough to see the full moon setting on the horizon. I settled easily into meditation, and I asked for the Father.

His brilliance appeared before me, and I wondered if my visit to Amma in Italy that summer had prepared me to consciously connect with His light. Possibly, Her work had led me to such an opening.

Just as that thought passed through my mind, the Father said to me, "You are correct." Then He suggested that I go to Amma and offer my gratitude.

I called on Her presence, and she immediately appeared before me. In deep gratitude, I bowed to Her. As my head was lowered, she pointed to the red stone in the very back of the etheric crown. She was letting me know that stone held her energy. I was very pleased.

As I lifted my head, I could see Amma giving me something energetically. I asked Her what She was doing and She did not respond. It was typical of Her not to speak very much in the etheric as in the physical.

I decided to tune in deeper, and upon doing so, I realized I was encircled by Divine feminine Masters. Amma sat directly in front of me, Mother Mary directly behind me, and the Goddesses of Wisdom and Peace on either side. There were others present, but I could not distinguish them, while it was clear they were all working together to perform a ceremony.

I tried to ask questions and intellectually understand what was happening, but it was to no avail. With every attempt to find answers, I would only feel a slight pain in my head. This had happened before in my meditations, and it signified that it was not necessary to intellectually understand all that was occurring. Possibly in a ceremony of all female Beings it was more important for me to feel than to think, since feeling is a more prominent, feminine characteristic.

Once I was content to drop into feeling, I had a wonderful time. It was amazing to be surrounded by Divine feminine energy. The beautiful Beings emanated streams of warmth, nurturance and love. I was encased in their light, and I felt myself melt into their brilliance. It was clear they were performing a ceremony to welcome me into the mother phase of life. They were celebrating with flowers, dance and prayer, much like human women celebrate a rite of passage with a wedding or a baby shower.

After a time, I called in my genetic mother to thank and acknowledge her for being with me through my maiden years. She appeared instantly in her human form, and she looked terribly uncomfortable. She seemed panicked as she viewed the female Beings around me and the ritual being performed.

I began to wonder how I could help my mother feel more comfortable when she suddenly dropped her human veil and appeared before all of us as the beautiful soul that she is.

She had a gift for me, and I held out my hands to receive the crystal I had given her that August for her fifty-fourth birthday. It was the first crystal that had ever been given to me, and its energy served to bring forth angelic qualities. Two months earlier, I had realized I was to pass the crystal on to my mom, and so I did. As she handed it to me in the meditation she said, "I have always known who you are. I have never forgotten." As I heard her message, I began to cry with relief. The pain of past rejection emerged from my eyes, and I could feel human tears roll down my cheeks.

My mother invited me to put the crystal into my heart, and she said, "You are truly an angel." I continued to sob as grief poured out of me and joy poured in. Then I asked my mom why she had been so angry at me for following my spiritual path. She responded that she had never been angry as a soul, but as a human mother she had fear.

I knew she had been embarrassed by my spiritual adventures, and I asked her in that moment if she was proud of me. I wanted her to gush with pride as human mothers sometimes do. She did not. She simply said, "Of course. We are *all* doing God's work." Then she proceeded to remind me that she had served her role exactly as we had agreed to before we came to earth. As a soul, she had never forgotten who I was, but as a human mother she pretended to forget.

I thanked her deeply as I remembered the perfection in it all. Then I told her I wanted for us to commune in the physical world as we were in that moment, as two beautiful souls rather than struggling mother and daughter. She said we would again. I asked her when that would be, and she said, "Maybe it is not too far off." I was still crying and I begged her to come with me on the spiritual journey. She responded exactly as she had as a human mother when I had pressed her spiritually. She said sternly, "Do not push me." I continued to cry, and she said gently, "Love me. Love me." I told her that I did love her and I wanted her to come with me.

As I spoke, I was intensely aware of the magnificence of my

mom's soul. Her light was so brilliant it was almost blinding. I could also see her physical body and personality waiting off in the distance. I looked at her physical being and I said to her soul, "I cannot pretend to be part of that world anymore."

She said, "Yes, I know, and I mourn you as my daughter." I continued to sob as she turned to her right, toward Amma, and said, "You have your Mother now."

Our communion continued for some time. Much was said, and much I do not remember. When we felt complete, her soul began to turn toward her human body. I reminded her that as a human mother she would have the crystal that was in my heart, and she said, "Yes. I know."

Then I saw my mother's glorious, Divine soul begin to squeeze itself back into her human form that was contracted with the darkness of fear. "Mom, don't!" I yelled, but she did not honor my cry. The sight was so painful I could not bear to watch, and I instantly opened my physical eyes to leave the meditation.

I slowly and methodically moved my fragile body to rest on the floor. I lay in complete stillness with my eyes fixated on the ceiling while my cells began to integrate all that had occurred in those few minutes of meditation.

Unveiling Truth

For the following period, I found myself constantly surrounded by feminine Masters. Amma was always directly in front of me, and Mother Mary was always behind me. It was both beautiful and overwhelming. I assumed they were working with me energetically, but since Amma was leading the process, no explanations were offered.

My lessons during this period seemed to come more from daily life experiences than from my meditations. One lesson evolved around my continuing clothing saga. As my journey progressed, it became clear that it was time for me to release more clothes from my previous lifestyle.

I gathered all that was left of my business attire. I tried on every piece, and while they fit physically, they no longer fit emotionally or spiritually. I decided I would bring them to the beautiful angel who owned the second-hand clothing store in Santa Fe.

That weekend, the owner of the yurt I rented came to town. I wanted to show off my designer clothes before I released them, and so I told her she could look through the box and choose one or two pieces to keep as a gift from me. When I brought her the large box of clothes, I knew my intention was to boast more than it was to give. It felt wrong, but I did not alter my plan. Then, just before she left town, she returned the box to me.

The following morning, I opened it to see what she had

chosen. When I looked inside, I was horrified to find that almost everything had vanished! All of my prize designer brand names, my beautiful dresses and the last of my professional clothes were gone! Only my torn college sweatshirt and a ratty T-shirt remained. I could not believe it.

I took a walk to clear my head, and I only became more agitated. I returned home to meditate. Once I shut my eyes, I received the message loud and clear. My energy had been arrogant, and the loss of my clothing was the universe's response.

All I could do was cry. I did not cry for the lost clothing, I cried in gratitude. I was grateful to see another layer of false pride had arisen to be healed, and I felt blessed that the consequence of my unclear action was so small. My mantra became, "Thank you God for teaching me this lesson so gently." As tears streamed down my face, I prayed that all of my arrogance would be healed. I called in every powerful light being I could think of and I asked for their help.

Then, I began to build an altar to humility. I moved through my tiny home to gather symbols of false pride. I ripped the University name off my torn college sweatshirt and the amount of money I had helped raise for charity that was embossed on the old T-shirt. As I set these symbols of material accomplishments on the altar, for the first time I understood that the Divine carried me through the successes I treasured, and I could not take the credit. I realized that my so-called accomplishments were simply experiences that led me back to spirit. They were not, nor had they ever been, anything more than that.

As I continued to place symbols of false pride on the altar, I knew that every moment of my life had been guided by spirit.

Divine direction does not begin when one consciously opens to it, but the grace of spirit is the guiding force in every moment of existence.

I felt deeply humbled as I gazed at the completed altar, and I asked the Father to direct me to take it down only after I had completely released the layer of arrogance. To my request, I received the most precious response. I was told that because my prayer was so sincere, it was immediately answered. The moment I had completed the altar, the healing had taken place.

My heart overflowed with gratitude. "Father, I love you," I gushed in response to the emotion surging through my being. He seemed genuinely moved by my outburst of affection. It was almost as though He blushed just as most humans do when someone sincerely expresses their love. I was surprised, and I said to Him, "Father, You are *so* human."

"No, my child," He responded gently, "It is *you* (the human race) who are so Divine."

Heaven to Earth

As I continued on my journey with the feminine Masters, I began to reflect on my spiritual path. At that point in my evolution, I had passed through seven spiritual thresholds, each representing one of the seven major chakras. Giving away all that I had evoked the final of these clearings. Each passage had been massive, and as I had muddled my way through, I had many moments of wondering if I would survive each one.

The last few years had felt like a constant process of peeling away all that I had been taught was truth. I had left behind just about everything I was raised to hold dear. I had left the academic world, the professional world and my family values. I had left men I loved and money I believed kept me safe. I had lived through a perpetual test of hearing Divine guidance and making the choice to follow all that I knew to be true in my heart, even as fear coursed through my veins.

As I had passed through each doorway and the gifts were showered upon me, it was easy to see the grace in it all. But there was always a period of extreme darkness just before the end of each tunnel, when all of the fear was making its final attempt to be honored, and I wondered if I would make it to the clearing.

The beings of light who accompanied my journey knew it was my prayer that others would pass through the tunnels with more ease than I, just as my path had been smoothed by those who had come before me. So whenever I contemplated quitting the entire spiritual process, they were quick to remind me that every moment one person honors truth, it becomes easier for every other person that walks on this earth to do the same.

In my search for that which could fill me, I had honored my guidance, and time and time again, the world of spirit graced me with love, generosity and blessings. Along the way, I came to realize that my role, like all others, is to bring the seemingly separate worlds of spirit and matter together.

While I had been gifted with a beautiful connection to the spiritual world, I could feel that my true work would be rooted in the physical. The importance of my life would be in bringing the grace of the heavens to the earth plane and to all of us who walk upon Her.

Christmas Day

The sun rose to touch the tips of the high mountains, and I awoke to the final day of the retreat. With great expectation, I entered into meditation on Christmas morning.

As the etheric world came into focus, I saw above me the most glorious sight of the heavens opening. Wondrous white clouds parted and I was raised to enter the gateway that was offered. I found myself immediately in the brilliant crystal city I had visited with the Father. Every structure was made from crystallized grace, and it offered the most radiant glow of truth in form.

An Ascended Master who was the keeper of the city greeted me with tremendous love. Together we walked through the crystal streets, and He led me to a grand feast. While He sat at the head of a long table, I sat just to His left. The table was lined with other people who I imagined existed in physical bodies. I quickly glanced at the others, but I did not recognize any of them.

As I observed all of us engaged in laughter and celebration, I wondered why the Christ was not present. It was Christmas day, and I assumed it would be Jesus who would greet me in my meditation.

I focused my human will so I was able to ask the question in the etheric, "Is this celebration for the Christ?"

My question was received with bewilderment.

"It's Christmas day, " I explained, "Are we together to celebrate the birth of the Christ on the earth plane?"

Upon asking the question, I realized that in the etheric realm there is no time or space, no definition and no limitation. Every day is Christmas, and every moment exists to celebrate the Divine.

the blessings of england

A Reunion with Angels

As the retreat came to a close, a prayer of mine was answered. The beautiful British couple I had met at Amma's were celebrating their thirtieth wedding anniversary, and they sent me a plane ticket so I could participate in the festivities. Four days after Christmas, I arrived in England to visit Anne and Michael.

Since returning from Amma's, I had kept an account of my meditations and much of what I learned in letters to the couple. Their presence was a critical part of my retreat. I often felt overwhelmed by all that was unfolding, and as I wrote to them of my experiences, the fear dissipated and the love revealed itself. I usually felt an experience was only complete after I relayed to them the gifts that had been offered.

It was a tremendous blessing to be with them once again. We had shared so much through letters and in love, and yet we had only spent a few hours together in Italy.

When I first arrived, I was amazed to see their home which lies just outside of London. It is decorated with relics from old churches and temples. A statue of the Hindu God Shiva greets visitors at the door, and a massive wooden cross hangs above the marble fire place in the living room. A crystal Buddha accompanies guests on the back porch and pages from an ancient Koran are encased in the study. To me, the magical six bedroom house is a cross between a shrine and a home.

Before I arrived, I wondered if the three of us would enjoy each other's company. We had bonded through our spiritual quests, yet we led very different lives. They were still an older British couple and I was still a young American.

Within our first few hours together, Anne, Michael and I talked and laughed about some of our spiritual adventures and misadventures, and the laughter continued throughout my two week stay. Our energies and differences balanced each other very well, and it was wonderful to be together. I found Anne to be one of the most grounded and devoted people I had ever known, while I discovered Michael to be one of the most eccentric. Under their conservative facades, they both loved the unusual and the extraordinary. Their lives were not filled with conservative older couples as I had imagined, but their home overflowed with individuals from all different countries and backgrounds. The common thread that ran throughout their home and their visitors was a devotion to the Divine.

The anniversary celebration was a grand occasion as family and friends arrived from all parts of England and the world. A master violinist filled the air with grace, while all of us talked, laughed and feasted on traditional British cuisine. I met most of Anne and Michael's family in that one day, and I was grateful to be welcomed so graciously. As various guests toasted the couple, I learned much about them, and I realized they had deeply touched the lives of many people.

Remembrance of Grace

The English countryside was a sharp contrast to the American Southwest. While the high desert was dramatically stark and dry, the air in England was moist and the earth rolled gracefully with soft hills. There was a gentleness in the land that was rare in the high desert, and the environment seemed to radiate a feminine quality.

A few days after the anniversary celebration, Anne and I drove through the rolling hills to the sacred site of Avebury. On this land, centuries before the birth of the Christ, huge stones were placed in three circles in worship of the Divine. As we approached the formation that remains, I was disappointed to find that many of the stones had been hauled away and all that was left was not particularly beautiful to my eye.

While we walked through the site, I felt more irritable than tranquil. "Isn't it wonderful?" Anne remarked, and I remember thinking I should be impressed. Yet, I could not sense the sacred history of the land, and as my agitation only heightened, I found myself more interested in the other visitors than in the gray stone slabs.

After walking through the site, we chose to rest awhile on a grassy knoll. It was only when I lay on the ground that I received the blessing of Avebury. The moment my body touched the earth, I could feel the sacred land absorbing from me the internal turmoil that had begun to brew on our drive over. A dissonance had arisen, and as my body was held by the earth, it miraculously drained away.

Once the energy released, I offered my gratitude to the Mother and I asked about the nature of the healing. She explained I had been born and raised in a country that was based in rebellion. The United States was formed by those who had separated from their native land. Since I had been born in the States, I held in my cells a reverence for defiance. Yet, as my life unfolded, I had chosen to venture down a path of devotion to the Divine. The historic rebellion and the truth of devotion created a conflict within.

For years, Avebury had been a site of worship to the Divine, and it held an energy of acceptance for reverence. As I lay on the soil, my cells absorbed the remembrance of that grace, and the internal turmoil dissipated.

A Dying Flame

Another day, as the sun's rays filtered through the low clouds, Barbara, who had introduced me to Anne and Michael, brought me to Stonehenge, the beautiful temple of rocks that is famous throughout the world. The medieval phrase 'Stonehenge' means 'hanging stones,' and the formation towers dramatically on the wide sweep of Salisbury plain. As we approached what had once been another sacred site of worship, I was struck with the physical beauty of the remains. Tall stone slabs arranged in a circle frame the expanse of nature on all sides.

The creation of Stonehenge began around 2800 BC when huge stones, some as high as twenty feet, were brought from a great distance. They were presumably carried by raft on sea and river, and then dragged on rollers across country. The grandeur of the formation offers a testament to the power of devotion. The stones are aligned to point to sunrise at midsummer and sunset in midwinter, and it is believed Stonehenge was the site of sun-worshipping ceremonies.

After walking around the exquisite structure, I was excited to meditate. I expected an even greater healing than in Avebury since Stonehenge was more spectacular in appearance and in known history. I lay on the earth and closed my eyes. As I tuned into the earth beneath me, I was surprised to feel nothing. There was not a message or a miraculous healing. In fact, the energy felt dead. Immediately, I realized the site had been depleted.

With that thought, the Mother appeared to me and explained that many people have traveled to Stonehenge to admire its fame rather than its true power. Millions had visited the site without reverence for the Divine, and they took energy from the formation without giving anything back. As a result, the power of the site had almost completely dissipated.

As She spoke, I received an incredible lesson. I began to understand that unconscious energy is not neutral. When we are not aligned with the Divine, we actually steal energy from the space around us. We do not leave our surroundings unaffected, but depleted. Meanwhile, when we are aligned with the Source, we naturally give to our surroundings. So at every moment, we are either giving to or taking from our environment, but we are never neutral.

The Perfect Plan

After our visit to Stonehenge, we traveled further west to Glastonbury, a town rich in history, myth and legend. The village rests at the foot of Glastonbury Tor, a grassy hill rising over five hundred feet. At the top of the tor stands the remains of a tower which is all that is left from St. Michael's Church, which collapsed after a landslide in 1271.

According to legend, the area was once Avalon, the mystical site of Goddess worship. As Barbara and I hiked up the steep tor, I felt an amazing sensation of familiarity and comfort flood my cells. While we were blessed by the views across the Vale of Avalon, bliss flowed through my body and I only knew a resounding feeling of absolute grace.

Once we reached the top, I lay on the sacred earth and stared at the sky above. As I watched the clouds dance into various formations, it dawned on me that the Divine had directed my entire life so I would be lying on that tor, staring at that sky at that very moment. Six months earlier, I would have never imagined or dreamed I would be visiting England, which was a country I had once sworn never to return to. Yet the Mother had carried me back. As I pondered the perfection of the Divine Plan, I fathomed that the process of my life would continue to unfold in Divine grace, and my greatest decision was to find pleasure or pain in the adventure. Yet, regardless of my bliss or battle, the journey would continue forth.

Tears of Grace

The remainder of my two week stay was spent in the London area. I loved The National Gallery, and for days I returned to gaze at Piero della Francesca's painting of *The Baptism of Christ*. I was entranced with the light that radiated from the depiction of Jesus standing in prayer as John the Baptist blesses Him with holy water. I stood before the painting for so long that the security guard kindly offered me his chair that was positioned in front of the masterpiece. I sat absorbing the light of God, and feeling that I never wanted to leave that simple space.

Of all the blessings my trip to England offered, it was my connection to Anne, Michael, Barbara and their families that was the most profound. The greatest adventure rested in getting to know each of them. I was deeply touched by their warmth and the brilliance of their love.

When my amazing journey in England was complete, Anne and Michael brought me to the airport. As my flight prepared to board, I could not prevent my tears from flowing. I cried in gratitude for their beautiful presence in my life, for the gifts of England, and for the absolute grace of the Divine.

*enraptured in
emptiness*

Nothing for Everything

I returned home to a New Mexico warm spell. Only vague hints of the winter storms remained and the sun shone gallantly over the high desert in early January. On my first night back, I crawled into bed and pondered emerging from the womb I had known. The retreat was over, and it would soon be time to return to the material world and a more interactive existence. As I contemplated the change, I prayed I would retain my conscious connection to the Divine even outside the serenity of the round home and my quiet life.

I felt fearful about leaving the comfort of the retreat as I thought about how I would support myself once again. As practicality reared its head, I ruminated over what I would have to offer upon my return. I pondered the question intensely.

I realized that I knew how to follow the call of spirit, but I had not been given any particular skills for material work or any direction for my future. I could see into the world of angels, but I did not have artwork to display or poetry to read. I could travel through time and space, yet I was not a healer, a teacher or anything at all.

Terror began to grip me as I recognized that in the past I would have had much to offer. I used to be filled with accomplishments, plans and knowings. Now I lay in a small home with absolutely nothing. My past no longer seemed to be mine and so I could not carry it forth. The future appeared to be nonexistent and the present only offered the most resounding sensation of emptiness I had ever known. I began to cry as I realized the breath of the Divine carried with it all that I had once treasured.

As fear raged, I searched frantically for something I could give. I longed to find a material strength I could offer. I prayed to discover a talent I could share or a plan worth following. With every question I posed to myself, I only received a deepening feeling of nothingness.

As I continued to delve into the emptiness, my pain was dramatically heightened by my mom's voice ringing in my ears. As relentlessly as a fire spreads on a windy day through a dry forest, her alarm echoed through the ethers: "You are throwing your life away! You are throwing away everything!"

I began to sob hysterically and I continued my desperate search. After minutes or maybe hours of torment, I came up with two traits I knew I had: I could talk to the Divine and I could leave anything.

I felt devastated as I realized these two traits were not ones that were valued in the material world. Who would care that I could leave anything, and why would another believe I could speak with the Divine? Yet this was all that I had.

My tears continued to fall as the moon swept across the sky, and I knew my mom was right. I had thrown away everything! I had absolutely nothing to give, and all I had in that moment was a vexing sensation of nothingness filling every cell of my being.

In an instant of horror, I realized that in the nine months since I had consciously communed with the Mother of All Things, I had been stripped of everything I thought I knew, everything I believed and everything I felt I had accomplished. Not only had I given away my material possessions, but I had given away my life. I had surrendered my plans to the Divine, and now there was nothing left. Absolutely nothing.

In a moment of exhaustion laced with despair, I drifted off to sleep. A couple of hours later I awoke, and the tears immediately began to flow from my tired eyes. I felt deeply sad that I had nothing to offer. I had thrown my life away, and my only question was how to begin again.

In my pain, I decided to turn to the beloved Masters for help. They would surely carry me out of the darkness. I would tell them of my regret, and ask them to lead me back to a path of sanity and control.

I closed my eyes and prayed for a connection. Soon the Masters came into focus and I noticed they were surrounding me in a circle. To my complete surprise, they were all celebrating!

A surge of anger raged through me as I felt shattered by their lack of concern, but then a glimmer of hope appeared. It dawned on me that if the Masters were celebrating, there was indeed a reason for celebration. Possibly something magical was arising from the fire engulfing my being.

Just as that thought passed through my mind, the Mother's first words flashed in front of me with the brilliance of a bolt of lightning filling the night's sky.

"You are NOTHING without Me!" She seemed to rage.

In desperation and confusion I called on Her presence. She instantly appeared before me in absolute radiance. She came in the form of a woman with every color of light emanating from Her center. It was the most brilliant and beautiful display of the Divine I had ever seen.

I gazed upon Her in all of God's glory as She too celebrated my state of being, and I looked upon myself as I appeared next to Her. Just to the right of the most beautiful form I had ever known, I saw myself as a pile of plain, gray ashes. I sat in a heap, completely destroyed.

I lay in bed as horror engulfed me. I had no more questions. I only held one prayer, which I repeated over and over again, "Please God, help me!" I opened my physical eyes with the hope it would mitigate the pain. I could not bare to see the image of my life as ashes.

In a desperate search for relief, I carried myself to the front porch and into the cold morning air. My frantic breath matched my energy, and I began to walk.

With great force and determination, I traversed the dirt roads of the mountain village. I did not know where I was walking nor did I care. I simply could not stay still. I passed beyond the houses, and soon only the mountain stood before me. With terror lurking behind me, I began making my way up the steep terrain. I recklessly passed around bushes, over logs and even through a small stream. There was no path set out before me, only the one I created.

I had not even made it to the first clearing when I began to stumble from exhaustion. The futility of my attempted escape began to dawn on me, and I collapsed on the muddy earth. Tears streamed down my face and desperation coursed through my veins as I entered once again into meditation. While an endless void engulfed my being, I ventured to the etheric world to find the Divine Mother dancing around me. She was singing as She placed beautiful flowers around my neck and showered me with petals of Divine grace.

I still did not understand the reason for celebration, and all I could feel was emptiness. "Mother!" I cried, begging for Her to listen to the words I would speak.

"Yes, my child?" She responded in complete love as She came directly before me in all of Her radiance.

I gazed upon Her beauty, and I felt desperate to tell Her my truth. In a tone of complete honesty and equal simplicity, I said to Her, "Mother! I have NOTHING to offer .... NOTHING!"

As I spoke, the Father's voice echoed through the heavens. In a familiar tone, I heard Him say once again, "Leave your bowl completely empty so I may fill it completely."

With His words, I suddenly realized that since I had communed with the Divine Mother, not only had I given away my material possessions, but much more importantly, I had peeled away layers of false pride, limited beliefs, and an absolute determination to control destiny. I had relinquished an erroneous sense of security only to place my fate where it had always rested -- in the hands of the Divine. Every false belief, every old pain, every bit of fear and every limitation I had released simply created more space for the grace of God to flow through.

My path had been one of shedding illusion, and now I lay absorbed in the realization that I had been stripped down to nothing. All that was left inside was a space to be filled. As a sense of wonder began to move through my veins, I watched the Mother of All Things joyfully re-enter her dance of celebration. Then She spoke these words I will never forget:

"Now, my child, you have EVERYTHING to offer."

reflections
three years later

Reflections

Upon completing the first draft of this book and sharing it with others, I came to realize that my adventure relates an archetypal journey. My original fear in recounting the story was that people would not believe my experiences, especially since I myself would not have done so even a short time ago. However, the initial feedback on the manuscript astounded me. "I completely related to the experience," I heard over and over again. "That was my story too," others would say.

My first thought was that these people experienced similar meditations. "Do you see the Divine Mother as well?" I asked, astounded that my best kept secret may not be so uncommon.

"No, I have never even meditated," many would say. Or I would hear regularly, "I have been meditating for years but have never received a vision." The responses came from a group so varied that it included a nineteen-year-old waitress who loves to party, an entertainment executive who lives in the heart of Los Angeles, an elderly woman who rarely leaves her home and a playboy who rarely leaves women.

I was amazed to realize that as varied as our lives may seem, we all share the same story. We all receive "visions" although they may not come in the classic form present in this adventure. They may come through a longing in our heart, a knowing in our soul, or in words whispered by a child. We are all guided every moment, even when we feel lost in the storm. And we all have moments of doubting that which we know to be true in our soul.

⌒

In the early days of my journey, when I was first discovering the world that lay beyond the physical dimension, I was tormented with the desire to honor the spiritual while it seemed there was no place for it in the physical. How could the spiritual lessons and teachings hold true in a human world filled with fear, anger, greed and horror?

The first teachings I received a few years before this story began seemed ludicrous. I was told that love is the only eternal force, and all fear is simply an illusion. My mind raged with doubt at the mere suggestion of such a reality, while my heart quietly sang its praise. I wanted it to be true, but did that make it true? I longed to know a world of pure love where I was eternally safe, always watched over and forever cherished. But could the human existence so obviously filled with pain have the force of love ruling its every move? Again, it seemed absurd, and again in my heart, I longed to have the courage to believe.

As my inner knowing begged me to explore another way, I began my spiritual quest. The first steps were the most treacherous as I felt like a new born fawn learning to walk while the world of fear screamed of impossibility, danger and humiliation. I decided to leave my well paying job in the city and move to an eccentric retreat center that focused on spiritual growth and healing. It was horrifying to try to find my balance on new legs while the winds of chaos and uncertainty raged around me and within me. It was especially terrifying since I did not know that the hand of spirit was guiding my every movement. I did not realize I was being watched over and that every instant I was safe in the arms of the Divine. It was only in taking the first step and then another and another that I came to experience more fully the grace of spirit. In time I began to realize that it is indeed the force of love that rules this planet.

CO

In the beginning, my inner knowing did not present itself in a spectacular fashion. The Christ did not appear before me and espouse the wisdom of the heavens. The Divine Mother did not present Herself throughout my day. The guidance was much simpler. It was present in the moments of longing I felt when I tried to dress for a job I no longer wanted. It was in the excitement that coursed through me when I ventured into the unexpected. It was in my prayers that I cried without tears to a God I was not sure existed. They were not astounding moments, and they would have made a much simpler story, yet it still would have been the same tale. It would have been a tale of a young woman doing her best to honor the call of her heart and the knowing in her soul, even while fear raged within her and outside of her. It would have been a story of adventure, excitement, torment and fear. As she would venture to follow her inner knowing, her fear would arise to be cleared, and there would be moments of wondering which force would win out.

Then, after many trials and miracles, the darkest moment would pass, and the light of truth would shine forth more brilliantly than ever before. The truth of spirit would win out, because that is the end of every story.

⚬

In the three years since I have lived this adventure, my journey continues to unfold in excitement, brilliance, pain and love. The two worlds that once seemed so separate continue to meld together, and I have come to have an even greater appreciation for the lessons and truths that have been given to me by the world of pure spirit.

While the details of my journey will always vary, my quest remains the same: to have the courage to follow my truth while illusion screams in rebellion. Each and every moment I am still faced with the same choice. Do I honor the rage of fear or the call of love? Do I follow a familiar path of limitation or the one that promises nothing except change? Do I step where I have always walked or do I leap into a void so vast I cannot see the end?

Some moments I honor my heart's cry, and other times I still walk into the jaws of illusion. And while the miracles only grow in brilliance, in a sense, so too does the darkness. As I clear away deeper and deeper layers of fear, the illusion that arises is even more dense. Yet so too is my remembrance of the light, my faith in the Divine and my knowledge of the power of love. And in those moments of illusion when I call to spirit and I do not feel a response, I try to remember that it is in the times of greatest darkness that the greatest transformations occur. It is in the moments when all seems to be lost that something has left us which has not yet been replaced: a fear that no longer suits us, a limitation that we have allowed to slip away, an illusion that we no longer hold dear to our hearts. And while we feel paralyzed by the darkness, it is that very void that allows the most powerful change to take place. For in that moment of nothingness, our only hope is for a higher grace to fill us. It is only when we release our tight grasp on the reins of fate and we have the courage to fall into the seemingly endless void that the Divine can catch us, and we can be filled with the miracle of spirit. For only when we are willing to risk, will we receive the rewards of another way.

∞

While the spiritual journey continues to challenge me, the graces on the path are undeniable. The blessings that have been bestowed upon me, the friendships and intimacy I have known, the laughter that has coursed though my being, and the love that is the undeniable presence of spirit are far greater than the gifts the illusion of fear only promises. And fear never delivers. The illusion pledges to keep us safe, yet it is only the truth of love that offers us safety. Fear vows to shelter us from loneliness, but it is the very force that prevents true intimacy. It boasts that it will answer our every prayer, yet it does not even know the truth of our longing. It begs us to follow its course, yet in doing so we will only know more despair, more loneliness and more longing.

flames *of* grace

While fear continues to rage, love forever calls to us from the depths of our being. It whispers to us through the longing in our heart and the knowing in our soul. It hails us in the breeze that flows through the branches and the bird's song that fills the morning air. It showers down upon us as snow in winter and heat in summer. Yet it never demands that we follow. It simply offers us another way.

The choice forever remains in our hands.

Blessings on your journey.

Acknowledgements

It is with tremendous pleasure and humility that I acknowledge the grace of spirit that has guided these experiences, created this book and has blessed my every step. In gratitude I offer my life.

It is with equal pleasure that I acknowledge the thinly disguised angels who have walked with me on this earth plane and have filled my life with the remembrance of the Divine, the hope of the heavens and the faith of all things.

My precious friends. Barbara Upton who was my first spiritual teacher and remains a golden anchor in my sometimes turbulent sea of growth. Michele Muir whose talent exemplifies brilliance. Lynn Edwards who reminds me that every view along the way is equally spectacular. Jean Frey whose laughter echoes through my soul. Brent Keltner who defines friendship in my life. Soad Kader for believing in my dreams simply because they are my dreams. Claudia Trembus for the strength of her light and the power of her love. Joy Franklin for teaching me integrity by living it. Uma, Lisa M., Kiersten, Andy, Mary and Alexis for the grace of their presence in my life.

Joanne and every yoga teacher who has blessed my path. Sharon, Audree, Pauqel and all of the great healers who have helped me along the way. Jon and the many friends and family who housed and fed me during my days as a spiritual waif.

Paulo Coelho for lighting my path with his faith. Emmanuel and Pat Rodegast for shining the light so brightly that I could not miss it. Shakti Gawain for her spiritual auto-biography that inspired me to honor my truth. Gloria for fanning my fire with her brilliance.

My family and all we have shared. Kathy for always being a safe place to turn. Jeff who is everything a sister wants in an older brother. Joan for her willingness to meet in the middle when our paths seemed to be heading in opposite directions. My parents and grandmothers for the gift of their love.

I am forever grateful to those who lived this story with me. Lisa who walks with me every step of the way. The British couple who carried me when I was too weak to walk and the angel who connected us. The incarnation of the Mother I visited and Her staff I terrorized. The families and individuals who welcomed me so graciously into their homes and who forever remain in my heart.

This book was created by the grace of God and the grace of all of the friends and family who lent their brilliance to this dream. Thank you for all of the hours editing, copy-editing, and designing this work. I am awed by your talent and generosity. Jerry Snider, Michael Langevin and the Magical Blend staff offered incredible support for this book, even before it went to press, which inspired me to leap once again.

My gratitude to all of those who continue to walk with me.

If you would like to be on the Sacred Flame Publications
mailing list to be apprised of new releases and events in your
area, please send your name and address to:

Sacred Flame Publications
Mailing List
PO Box 3077
Sedona, AZ 86340